Eleonora Duse
Let Me Have My Wings

a novel

by

John Passfield

Rock's Mills Press
Oakville, Ontario
2021

Published by
Rock's Mills Press

Cover Design: Craig Passfield
Cover Illustration: A photograph of Eleonora Duse, in Venice, in 1894, when she was 36 years old. She met the poet, Gabrielle D'Annunzio, in 1895, when she was 37 and he was 32.

The novel to which the main character refers is *The Flame* (*Il Fuoco*), by Gabrielle D'Annunzio, which was published in 1900.

Chapter 1

Waiting to go on stage as Hedda. I am already Hedda, but thinking and feeling my way more deeply into the part. Checking to see that the pistol is in the right place. Last night I almost shot Judge Brack. He said he could see it in my eyes. He told me – after the curtain – that I should ease my performance back. He said that Sarah would have winked with her upstage eye. I told him that Sarah could never be Hedda. I told him I had good reason to shoot him – some night I might actually do so and that would be that.

A woman's story at a winter fire.

Alone and cold. It is quiet and it is dark. Shivering under the thin blanket. Waiting for my mother and father to come back. This hotel room is cold. No money for candles or coals. They are acting in a play. The theatre is warm and bright and clean. Oh how I long to grow up so I can act on the stage.

There is life

A story that begins in Vigevano.
A story that begins in Verona.
A story that begins in Venice.

in every performance

I understand that you were born near Vigevano?
And that you were born into a troupe of travelling actors?
Do you have a special attachment to that place?

of every play.

The last twilight of September.
The campanile of San Marco.
The campanile of San Giorgio Maggiore.

I arrive quietly in a town. I bundle up so no one can see me. I avoid the crowds at the station. I shun all requests for interviews. I ride in a blind-drawn carriage. I set up my shrine in a hotel suite. The maids are instructed that I need my quiet and my rest.

Images of an ideal life.

My legs are being whipped. A birch switch. The pain is quite intense. I am only four years old. I am about to go on the stage. I can feel the tears that are welling up in my eyes. I will be sure to give a good performance tonight.

There was a young girl who lived in a castle.

"There is something strange about La Duse these days."
"Is she sometimes bored with the most successful of her roles?"

A child was left
alone
in the desert.

Brain was racing - bait and switch - dangle on a peg - live my life over - smashed on the kitchen floor - reluctant to move - while sunlight dances - looking out my window - almost afraid to ask - deeper into myself.

An article about that novel! – what is it called? – *The Flame*! Well tell me why on earth would you come to me? There is no connection – whatsoever – between that novel and my life!

No! – absolutely not! No! – I have never read it! Nor do I ever intend to read it! – not even one scurrilous page!

Yes, I have heard rumours! Yes, so-called friends have told me things! Now you come here – to me – and refer to it as 'a spot-light that is lighting up my life'!

Monday was washday at the castle.
The washerwoman hung the royal robes on the line.

I have no life of my own. I am only alive on stage. I Am Hedda, or Marguerite or Theodora or Cleopatra. I am these people and they are me. Outside the spotlight there is darkness. There is no such person as Eleonora Duse.

What law of heaven have I transgressed?

On a blanket with the other actors under a tree. Waiting for my father to come back from town. My mother handing out food from a meagre sack. Studying my part on a scrap of wrinkled paper. I am hungry, but I nibble at my portion of the bread and the cheese. If the child I will play will be hungry, so must I be.

There was a young lady who eloped with a storied soldier.

Being pestered for an interview.
Why can I not be left alone?

It looked
as if
it would not survive.

Nowhere else to go - he will take his place - have a favourite role - the secrets of the heavens - persisted an image - poised on a knife edge - i fall in the dust - alone and cold - don't make the mistake - between its fangs.

No! – this interview is over! – this interview will not take place! It doesn't matter what I tell you! – you did not come here for the truth! You could take and twist every word on the subject that I would say!

Why should I trust you? Why should I trust you? Why should I trust you to write the story as I tell it to you?

Why would you come to me? Did he send you? Did he send you to stir up publicity for his treacherous book?

A star was shining
in a corner of the sky.

Sometimes I go out for a walk. I bundle up so I cannot be seen. I am not the visiting actress come to town. I am a character in a role. Only a thread is holding that life. I barely see the sights as I walk along. I am that character drawing my breath as I walk along.
The pure spendour of innocent youth.
Walking beside the wagon – in a cramped and crowded dressing-room back-stage. Dreaming of the stages in Paris and London and Rome. Sarah Bernhardt taking her bows. She is Phedre, Cleopatra, Marguerite. She is standing on stage in St. Petersburg. The Czar is leading the applause. A hand on my shoulder – it is time to go on stage.

A story with its gains and its losses.
A story with its highs and its lows.
A story with its ecstasy and pain.

I study my scripts as they come to me. They are written in paper and ink. Where, in these words, is my name ever mentioned? Where am I in this time and this place? I think and I feel with the sharpest of eyes. I sit in the dark and absorb these words. The ink on the paper begins to melt and flow into my veins. I turn on the light and there is ink and blood on the page.

It is carnival time in Venice.
Everybody wears a mask.
I walk along beside the canals.
I look in the shops.

Your father and mother were actors as well?
And your ancestors were also prominent in that trade?
How far back, I wonder, are there actors in your family tree?

I am Juliet. I am fourteen years old. It is my fourteenth birthday today. We are on the outskirts of Verona. The old horse plods along – the wagon has a squeaky wheel.

It is tourist season in Verona.
Many tourists have come to the town.
I too have come to see what I can see.

There was a girl who was born in Vigevano. This girl was born to act. She was completely absorbed in every role she played. She transformed herself into each and every character. Every eye in every theatre was glued to the stage.

When the dark moods come on, they are persistent and they are un-kind. I lie prone and brood for hours. They are a heavy weight on my chest. The drizzle of rain here in the courtyard. As if a statue of myself has fallen on me.

A magnificent and unique festival.
The Hall of the Greater Council.
The Paradiso of Tintoretto.

Oh I hope that we don't meet in Heaven. If we do, God forbid – if you are the other half of my soul – it will be an extremely shallow eternity for me. You burned your candle here on earth. I saved mine for the after-life. How many candles does it take to light a room?

Hedda-Duse – Duse-Hedda – I am she and she is me. There is no exit from the stage. A nightmare at the deepest level of our mind. I cannot save Hedda – she cannot save me. Only a pistol-shot could jar the sleeper awake.
What is the natural measure of my sorrow?
Riding on the wagon. Moving from town to town. Seeing my name in the newspaper. 'The young girl who plays the waif is a fresh breeze.' Asking my mother what the newspaper means. Did I do good or did I do bad? Did the newspaperman like my acting or did he not? There would be nothing I could change – I was playing me.

There was a lady who felt she had danced herself tired.

"Duse as a woman is capable of great sacrifices and great heroism."
"She is a morbid egoist who, I would say, loves to suffer."

But the child
found
water, food and shelter.

The wine on everyone's lips - you could manipulate him - walks on desert sand - to keep control - consider your relationship - thinking, breathing, suffering - two muses in fact - how much of yourself - the furthermost depths of his being - between sunrise and sunset.

How do I know that I can trust you? How do I know that what you say is in the book? I have not read from that book even one false and deceitful word!

Look at my back! Look at my back! I am turning around for you to see!

What do you see? Just what do you see? It is a knife! – a butcher knife! – and that is my blood!

The young man climbed the ladder.
He was ruthless and he was cold.

Phedre on the streets of Buenos Aires. Marguerite on the sidewalks of New York. Medea or Electra in London in a hotel suite. Thinking, breathing, suffering, struggling. In a cocoon that she must break out of or she must die. Only half alive until the curtain goes up.

The soul of an ideal world.

Walking from town to town. Mother and I, side by side. We wear our costumes as we walk. We have no other clothes that we can wear. People call us vagabonds, but I am someone different every night. I am a maid when I wear an apron. I am a princess when I wear a lace shawl. When the queen gives an order, the heads of the peasants will roll.

There was a young wife and mother who lived in a doll's house.

Being pestered by my memories.
They come at me in a swarm.

It became
a desert-dweller

for the rest of its life.

The fading candle-light - will take their cue - a star and a lock - to become myself - the forces at work - essence of life itself - rather it were not so - rear and twist and plunge - all she knew - dwindles to a trickle.

And you have come to twist the knife! Is that your plan? One more scurrilous scrap of gossip for sale in those grubby stalls!

If I affirm – the tongues will wag! If I deny – the tongues will wag! I will never get out from under the weight of that book!

Oh – who let you in? Was the door not locked? Put your hat back on your head! – I will show you the door!

When the vintner turned his back,
the boy stole a basket of wine.

Why would I want to be myself? I am drained – completely drained – of all blood and flesh and bone – when I am on stage. I am bombarded by every sensation. Nourished by a sunbeam – crushed by a cloud. Every atom of my being is a coal in a fire – a child's balloon in a hurricane. I could not live both on and off the stage.

After I did that wrong, I could never make any believe me.

Approaching a big city. Father tells me it is merely a town. Getting the feeling that I have been here before. The apples in the orchards, the peasants in the fields. The river, the bridge, the shops that line the streets. I could tell my father where to turn as we come to the centre of town. He says we are heading for the out-door theatre. Surprised when he doesn't turn at the street where I used to live.

There was a dog

A story with sudden changes of direction.
A story with many beginnings and very few endings.
A story which continues on and on.

who would walk

And so you travelled throughout the small towns of Italy?
And you began your career – at what? – at four years old?
Any interesting incidents to relate from those times?

beside a wagon.

I have travelled all over the world. I have played every classical role.

I have played every great female character in the repertoire. Shakespeare – Ibsen – Racine. English – Norwegian – French. Now Wagner has established a theatre at Bayreuth. There are now German classical roles. Why do all these nations have all the great theatres? Oh why are there no great Italian classical roles?

Something in her that was vanishing.

Playing Juliet. In Verona. On my birthday. On the stage. The stage is my birthplace, my balcony, my tomb. A world of sunshine and rose-petals. An ancient coliseum and a make-shift platform. Juliet – alive and breathing – through smiles and tears.

Chapter 2

In a lull between tours. On the look-out for a temporary diversion. I am nothing when I am not on stage. Sitting on a balcony with friends, a glass of wine in my hand, while sunlight dances and sparkles on the waves. Desultory conversation, familiar topics, tired ideas. It seems like weeks now that I have been languishing in my cocoon.

The memory of a silent promise.

The three of us blown by the wind. Father, Mother and I. A series of rag-tag acting troupes. Rickety stages, patched costumes, battered props. Fierce rain, blistering sun, famine and feast. Learning my lines under the wagon as the rain beats down. Learning my lines by candle-light. I inhabit other worlds when I am on stage.

There is death

A young girl who relies on others for advice.
A puppet who lies in a corner for days and days.
A rocket bursting into splendour.

in every performance

Why do you not want to be interviewed by this young journalist?
Surely you could manipulate him to your heart's content?
Would you not easily be the one who is in control?

in every play.

The Gloria of Veronese.
The Traghetto Di San Gregorio.
An echo in the Grand Canal.

Twilight in September in Venice. The light flashed on the water beside the gondola. Angels shone from afar on the campaniles. The young poet had agreed to speak to the crowd at the festival. The great actress exalted the poet with utmost praise. He thought of the city, of the actress and of his hopes.

She became for him the ideal.

Making gems of the smallest of roles. A princess, a maiden, a bride. A wife, a duchess, a matron, a slave. From cast-member to dona-secunda. Pressing my nose against the glass. Reading reviews as I study my parts by candle-light. I am making my way in the theatre. Someday I will be the prima-dona of my own acting-troupe.

The young girl had a dream. She would nurse that dream each day. That dream was very simple. That things would turn out for the best.

"She is at home among veteran artists."
"In every play, she alone commands the stage."

"There was a breath of fresh air at the theatre last night. There was an actress who was only in town for a single performance. She was as human as other actresses are not. She eschewed the layers of makeup; she eschewed the elaborate dress; she eschewed the rattling jewelry that Sarah always wears. She played Marguerite Gautier as if the woman was real. She didn't strut and pose and turn Armand, during his speeches, so she, herself, would always be upstage. Her face was bare and her range of emotions was all that the audience could endure. She was a woman whose heart was breaking right there on the stage. I don't know how an actress can do it. How can she live these demanding roles? It is an entirely new kind of acting – so real that it doesn't seem like acting at all. For sure she was Marguerite Gautier to the life."

The one who is deciding - we are all their prisoners - tampering with the alignment - he snuffs the flame - a moment of perfect clarity - waiting to go on-stage - a special attachment - seen the tumultuous love - dreaming of the stages - i had good reason.

Oh – are you still here? You surprised me. I thought that you had left long ago.

Why do you linger on so? Do you have nowhere else to go? Don't you realize by now that I have nothing that I am willing to say?

You never told me why you came here. Of course, I never expected you to tell. That is why I said I would walk you to the door.

Shall I write your article for you? Shall I do what every interviewer has asked me to do? To tell them the meaning of my life and my career?

To tell them what to write about what they have seen with their own bare eyes? Is this your greatest role, Signora? Is this the role for which you will always be known?

Does this role place you ahead of Sarah? Do you or Sarah shine more brightly in the greatest roles? Just what are you to Sarah – and Sarah to you?

The Queen's robe disappeared from the royal clothesline.
The washerwoman was arrested and put on trial.

I try not to think of my daughter. I wonder what she is learning in school. To be a lady – to live a good life – to forget her past. Listen to the teachers – listen to their words. Read my letters and write to me of your love. Know that your momma always wants the best for you.

A small cavity in the marble.

Becoming attractive to the males. Males on stage – males in the audience – males on the street. What do these males want from me? What do I want from these males? All of life is a series of plays in which we choose – or are given – our roles. Determined that I will choose the roles that are right for me.

The young lady had a dream. She would nurse that dream each day. That dream was very simple. That things would turn out for the best.

In a lull between tours.
Sitting on a balcony with friends.

She rants and raves like a harpy. She refuses to go inside. Refuses to speak when spoken to – claims to know Agamemnon's future as well as his past. Such ridiculous revelations. How could a slave girl claim to know what no one else knows?

Underneath the layers of laquer - ask you to pay - see the justice - reach inside another person - firmly in his grasp - strip them bare - barred the door - busy living my life - my life upside down - refine our enterprise.

So – you want me to give you my thoughts? I – who have never given my thoughts to the public before? I – who have let my great roles be the voices that speak for me?

What a scoop this would be for you! 'Scoop' – is that the word? Is that the journalistic word for a stab in the back?

I pour my heart out for you? I give you my blood in a pool in your hand? And you pour it into the ink-well and then dip your pen?

How much would your newspaper pay for such a confession? How many lira could I hold right here in my hand? Simply for letting you into my bedroom and into my mind?

Does Sarah sell those ridiculous stories that everyone reads? The stories of her pet monkeys and her zebras and her baths in tubs of milk? Does she telephone this nonsense to you – in time for your pressing deadlines, of course – when she knows the news will be slow on a quiet day?

I have died more deaths than any of my heroines. Unlike Sarah, I die both on and off the stage. How does she manage the press that is being so cruel to me?

An eagle flew too high
and bumped the star
and knocked it down.

Barges passed them on the water. Applause echoed through the Grand Canal. She was a distinguished tragical actress – he a young poet on the rise. The poet spoke of his plans and his dreams – of the speech that he would give. Of how his talent was not enough – he had need of a muse. He intended to fill life's goblet to the brim. The piazza was now black with the waiting throng.

Enchantments woven into the rhythm of the oar.

A racehorse in a stable of cattle. A greyhound in a pack of curs. An actual woman on the stage among wind-up dolls. A quiet butterfly on the stage with bellowing frogs. I shall never be able to act until I control the entire play. I must have a troupe of my own. I must pick and train my cast. Every actor on the stage must serve the play.

A star and a lock on a door.
A person being praised for the wrong reasons.
A writer using his pen to get revenge.

Technique? – no, I have no technique. When I am on stage I am not an actress. These are not characters in creaking plays, written by Dumas-fils and Sardou. These are not moth-eaten parts that I draw from an old theatre-trunk. These are people who inhabit my body – inhabit my heart, inhabit my mind – when I am on stage.

Everyone I meet wears a mask.
Some are smiles and some are frowns.
No one says a word as they pass me.
Every mask leaves nothing visible but the eyes.

How many prominent people has he managed to interview?
Would he not be intimidated by your fame?
Would you not control the narrative of the exchange?

It is the first Sunday in May. I hold a large bunch of roses. I am in my Juliet-clothes. On the outskirts of the town. The people of Verona pause and stare from the fields.

There is a magic about Verona.
It is where Juliet lived and died.
Verona is not like any other town.

There was no limit to her talent. She could transform herself into every great female role. Shakespeare – Corneille – Racine. Dumas – Hugo – Rostand – Sardou. She made every role her own.

You stole from me all the light that surrounded my head. All the light that came down from the heavens and lit on me. Darkness descended on me. A darkness I had never imagined nor ever seen. I snuffed out the candle that I kept in the window and sat in the dark.

A cloud of creamy Buranesi laces.
The patroness of Burano.
Silvery ripples in the wake of a barge.

Oh I get tired of the same old roles. The flame burns lower each time I step on stage. Did ever woman act like this when not in a play? Sacrificing for oafish males? – clutching camellias and shedding tears? – hugging a tobacco-stenched bear with food in his beard? There is no romance in my life – there is no passion in my thoughts. My life has all the makings of a shallow play.
You will win what you deserve.
Mother ill – cold – a pauper's ward. Too ill to travel – blood on the handkerchief – a tearful farewell. We leave a few candles behind – a few pennies – a shawl. We'll be back as soon as we can – we will find a better place – we must go now.

The lady had a dream. She would nurse that dream each day. That dream was very simple. That things would turn out for the best.

"La Duse is a spell-binding actress."
"In the better roles she is always a better Duse."

"There is a little provincial actress who is making some waves in the theatre world. She has played some roles of note and has attracted quite a loyal following. She let slip, the other day, in an impromptu interview, that her dream is to follow in the footsteps of the great Sarah Bernhardt. Well, who wants to be the one to tell her? I didn't have the heart. Sarah is the queen of the theatrical world. Kings and princes, and even czars, have poured praise – and gold – on Sarah's stage. She has hard-bitten critics eating humble-pie out of her hand. Sarah acts in English and French. This little lady speaks only Italian. Can you imagine *La Dame aux Camellias* – a French play, acted in Italian, on an English stage? Does she know how high the climb, how steep the cliff? Should this pretty little provincial actress, clutching a handful of kindly small-town reviews, even dare to think of entering the lioness's cage?"

No rules in heaven - hearts are breaking - the bowels of the cave - reveal what is wrong - is perpetual spring - praised for the wrong reasons - this thought has grown - can see it in their eyes - what will happen to me - dip it in lambs-milk.

Oh – you are so eager to hear my confession. You would love to know what I think of this whole sordid business. Of that scoundrel who stole my purse and stole my heart.

Of whether I've read his salacious drivel. Fingers scorched as I turned each page. Of whether I see my face in the pool of his fetid dreams.

But no! – I will never speak out on that subject! – I do not caterwaul in the press! I am a mystery – I am an enigma – I am as silent as Sarah is loud! I will never rip open my bodice and show you my heart!

But wait a minute! – where are you going? Since you are here, you might as well sit down. You make me nervous, standing there. I will give you five minutes, and then – out the door!

First – though – we have to come to an understanding. I will ask you some pertinent questions before we proceed. Move your chair closer – let me look into your eyes.

I like to see a person's eyes. Though I admit, I've been fooled before. The question is – can I trust you? – there are many actors who have never appeared on a stage.

The young man climbed the ladder.
He threw the other climbers down.

The young poet reminded the actress that it was now Autumn. She had a vision of the summer – soon to be sunken and dead. She asked him if he had been thinking of someone else. She was worried about her age. She had inspired him in the past – right up to this moment – she knew she had – but his eyes stared off in the distance. She wondered whether she – an aging actress – was still an appropriate muse.

The movements of a silent dance.

Sarah Bernhardt has her own theatre. I walk beside a wagon and act in a field in a tent. She speaks the language of Dumas and Racine. When I go to London, I shall have to act in Italian – when I go to Paris, I shall have to do the same. Sarah is welcome wherever she plays – even the Russians speak English and French. All the great plays are in those two languages. What that is comparable does Italy have to show?

The young wife and mother had a dream. She would nurse that dream each day. That dream was very simple. That things would turn out for the best.

My mind drifting back to those early days.
Searching back through the rubble of those days.

Oh you must try on this mask.
Every carnival-goer has to wear a mask.
I have one here that I picked out for you.
Let me try it on for size.
I have decided that this mask is the absolute you.

The milk and the bread - the bowels of the cave - floated above the crowd - worldly wisdom and despair - i struggle a bit - the agonies of the world - find in the newspapers - the judge would control - his only legacy - rely on you for sustenance.

Have you ever met D'Annunzio? Do you know him? Have you had dealings – of any sort – with him at all?

Have you interviewed him for your – what do you call it? Your 'rag'? – your 'scandal-sheet'? Your 'record of the life of our times'?

Did he send you? Did he send you to interview me? Are you, perhaps, my final coffin-nail?

Are you willing to promise me that you will deal fairly with me? That if I tell you things – which, mind you, I am probably not going to do – you will report them faithfully – accurately – as I tell them to you? That your primary goal, in this exchange, is to discover – and report – the simple truth?

Of course, a child can lie and still not believe that he has lied – he simply crosses his fingers behind his back. And I can lie to you in the same way. Are you keeping your eyes on my hands as I speak to you?

Oh I wish I could read your eyes. They are so sincere – but I have seen that look before. Is this a dagger which I see – behind your back?

When the baker turned his back,
the boy stole a basket of bread.

A glimpse of the poet D'Annunzio. I look through the hole in the curtain as the audience arrives. Someone mentions that he is seated in the front row. He is very unprepossessing. Rather short, slightly balding, his only good feature, I would say, is his eyes. Everyone recommends his books. A poet so plain in appearance? Poets should be tall – should be handsome – this one has no presence or flair. No – I do not wish to meet him – do not add his name to those who are allowed backstage.

According to the eyes that looked at it.

Climbing up the ladder. Graduating to troupes which have their own theatres – father and I. Troupes in the cities – the larger towns – with a regular clientele. No more setting up at fairs – rickety stages and drunken cat-calls. An actual theatre – a home for my characters. There are people who go to the theatre every night.

The dog would walk

An actress who acts with just her eyes.
A woman who rages like the sea.
A fluttering shower of rose-petals.

under the wagon

By what means does Sarah manage to control the press?
Does she not appear to give frank interviews?
Is she not the shaping force behind every printed word?

when it rained.

The bells of San Marco gave the signal for the Angelus. The actress concentrated her thought. The indefinable thrill of serving a vehement and passionate soul. She thought of him as 'the image-maker' – her praise was the fuel that fed his flame. She had dedicated her life to his career. Their gondola was nearly at the dock.

Real forms obliterated by dream-figures.

'They will crush you in the shell.' Where have I read that pregnant phrase? I have seen talent strewn on the path as I trudge along. Through rainstorms, through blizzards, through hurricanes of despair. Through bogs and briars and deserts of indifference and disdain. Are you still here?, my tormentors ask, when the weather takes a turn, and I am there – cold and wet, but not discouraged – shaking the rain and the snow from my shoulders and plying my trade.

Chapter 3

I drift lazily through the canals of Venice. Just myself and the silent gondolier. The oar plying the water as we drift along. Listlessness as a phase. A need to refresh and renew. I feel a need for change – for growth – for the expansion of my endeavours. What door, I wonder – what portal – is waiting for my gondola to pass through?

Will you aid this hand of mine to lift the dead?

Confined by the roles I play. Waiting while the prima-dona speaks. Waiting to respond to the life that she is living as I wait for her to live. She is dull, so I am dull. I have no emotion except that soon I will answer the door. When will I get to be the centre of all the lines of emotion on the stage? When will all the lightning strike the ground at my feet? A sack of grain on a stage filled with sacks of grain.

A visit

An audience listening to a play in another language.
A restless woman standing on a dock.
An actress who appears to have no life.

to the region

So you toured the smaller centres with your parents?
Acting often, as I understand it, on an outdoor stage?
Riding or walking beside a cart with all your belongings?

of life.

Ancient paintings that retain their vivid colour.
The gallery of the Academia.
The First Bonifacio's Massacre of the Innocents.

Is it exhaustion of the mind or of the soul? I have worked hard all of my life so it cannot be exhaustion of the body. I have been earning my daily bread since I was four years old. I am the sole source of sustenance for an entire theatrical troupe. I get letters asking when we will tour again. I sit on my balcony reading a book and wondering the same. I am the old horse who pulls the prop-wagon, waiting under a tree.

Come, come, come, come. Give me your hand.

Marguerite Gautier once again. Sarah plays her as a mechanical wind-up doll. I play her when I arrive in a new city or town. The audience already knows the play – in English or in French. More willing to put up with Italian in something they know. What they expect is another Sarah. What they get is Marguerite – no Sarah at all.

The young girl's father was important in the kingdom. The young girl was neither a princess nor a queen. The young prince took a shine to the girl. Though both of them knew that he was out of her star.

"Eleonora Duse presents a vision of the ideal actress."
"She is courtly as a princess, sweet and gentle as a maiden."

The sunlight sparkles on the Grand Canal! It is the day of Carnival! A flotilla of gondolas ambulates up and down! I wear a mask, as everyone does! I swell the throng of the great parade! I go back to my little apartment at the end of the day!

There is no exit - climbs up the vine-stalk - they were blown away - nothing i could change - never told me why - the grit and the angst - a nightmare at the deepest level - not moth-eaten parts - languishing in my cocoon - wrap the entrails.

You're a reporter. You deal in words – you write with a pen. Ideas are the medium of your trade.

Now, I want to ask you something. What is the percentage of truth in each bottle of printer's-ink? What does the label on the bottle have to say?

You sit down at your desk – you dip your pen in ink. If one's thoughts are not pure, will the ink refuse to flow? Just what do we see when we look at the ink on the page?

A scaffold was erected in the courtyard.
The washerwoman was told that she was to die.

The same old roles – the same old roles – the same old roles. Plays come through my letterbox – people hand me scripts in hotels. The same old ink, the same old paper, the same old words. And the audiences – yes, the audiences. If I don't play something they already know, they don't want to watch.

If money were my sole object – money and applause – I could play Marguerite Gautier every night for the rest of my life.

Oh this burning fire! – it is creeping over me!

Cafiero is a writer. Handsome – distinguished – a man of the world. What these oafish actors try to be but cannot. We visit museums, the grand café, carriage rides, a kiss at dawn. Can I trust him? – does it matter? – is it love? – for him or for me? Better not to think of such things 'til the end of the play.

The young lady was an aristocrat in Venice. She enjoyed all the perks of the social scene. On the marriage-market she was a prize quarry. She had her choice of many a handsome young man.

Drifting lazily through the canals.
A need to refresh and renew.

Each year I wear a different mask! Each night I attend a different ball! The orchestra plays – the music swells! I take off my shoes and dance until the dawn! I dance with a prince or a duke or perhaps, the Doge! I go back to my little apartment as the music fades!

Feel rather than see - water it down again - bringing these words alive - far from the thunderbolts - little gift is ready - waves of despair - a collection of gems - there is no audience - to bury me alive - clutched a token.

And how could *I* tell *you* the truth, even if I wanted to? Do you think that all of my memories are of actual happenings? I have often wondered, but I am no longer able to tell.

We think with our memories, wouldn't you say? I imagine this to be true. We think with the things that have happened to us and what we have done.

And the point that I am making – I am sure you can follow me – and even leap ahead. The point that I am making is simply this. How can we think if we don't know what our memories actually are?

The star fell into a puddle
and sank into the mud.

Oh these handsome young gondoliers. Why can they not wield a pen? Why is the writing of roles for me such a chore? Do they never go to the the-atre? – have they nothing dramatic to tell? Oh these handsome gondoliers. Strong backs – dull brains – nothing more.

Belike this show imports the argument of the play.

We are so happy here in the country. We go outside and pick the flowers. Oh I had hoped to never see a camellia – ever again. The air is fresh and clean. If only this cough would go away. I am trying to forget what Armand's father had to say. Is that a horse I hear in the courtyard? How can I do what I know I must do? It will be right, but it will be wrong – it will be life but it will be death. How can I tell Armand what I have promised to say?

> *A crowd as a thousand-eyed monster.*
> *A poet with an older and a younger muse.*
> *A person whose spirit has been dissipated.*

I have newspapers delivered to my rooms. I never read them – why would I read them? I have never once been helped by any advice. Oh I glance at them once in a while – the odd paragraph or two – when I have nothing else to do – in the depths of a sleepless night. Their range is infinitesimal – I could write better squibs myself. The best I would paint more brightly – the worst I would colour more dark. To these writers the stage is the size of a miniature toy.

> *The shops are filled with masks.*
> *They are hanging on the walls.*
> *There is a mask for every occasion.*
> *There is a mask for every mood.*

Setting up and giving performances at fairs?
Gradually getting better and better parts in plays?
Eventually working your way up to be prima-dona?

My mother's name is Cappelletto. We are a family down on our luck. Very far from being a family of ladies and lords. We are a vagabond handful of actors. I feel a close bond with Juliet.

> *We walk along the cobbled streets.*
> *We are in the centre of town.*
> *The Capulets and the Montagues all lived here.*

Her family were theatrical people. She was absorbed from birth in the art. Generations of actors had formed her. She would immerse herself in the roles that she played. She became the character everyone saw on the stage.

You have nothing that I would want. Whatever attraction there used to be in your presence, or in thoughts of you – crackling pine logs, sparkling wines, fresh spring flowers in the fields – are now ashes, dregs and weeds in a heap in the yard. Buried under a layer of deep snow.

The green robe of a prostrate woman.
The dagger of one of Herod's soldiers.
Leaving one's spiritual vision behind.

If I were to take my heart out of my chest and put it on this table and take a knife and sharpen it on this emery-stone and then proceed to cut out all of the heartache and humiliation and disappointment and despair – what, then, would be left, of hope, of cheerfulness, of optimism, as the fuel which would take me across this room and out that door?

Only Ibsen understands women – only Ibsen in our time. I am thinking of staging a season of nothing but Ibsen plays. But the managers and impresarios all tell me it cannot be done. A Nora, once in a while – an occasional Hedda is welcome as well. But plays are entertainment – art in the theatre does not go well. Even you – Madame Duse – even you, even you – must be careful to offer a program which will pay the bills.
The deed must then be done by my own hand.
Word reaches me in rehearsal. It seems that my mother has died. Two actresses who walked together beside the cart. She used to leave me in a dark hotel-room while she went out on stage. Perhaps my tears will flow tonight – when I am on stage.
No healing god is here – there is no cure.
I go out on stage – the play must go on. I try to focus – I swim in a blur. The full weight of my thoughts and emotions presses me down. My best performance or my worst – I shall never know. My mother and I in the photograph. My mother and I under the wagon – torrential rain. My mother and I in our costumes, walking from town to town. She was the Nurse on the day I was Juliet.

You were Juliet, my child, throughout the whole performance.
Oh I am Juliet still, Mother. I am Juliet still.

The lady rode a fine horse around the town. She attended any number of fancy-dress balls. There were many who envied her social position. Many men had offered to see the lady home.

"Duse is Ophelia – she is Ophelia – Ophelia for sure."
"Five waves of applause as she finished her final scene."

I work at the shop that sells the dreams! People come to Venice to buy! It is here that every life takes on a new sheen! I am saving up my money! I have my eye on another fine mask! I go back to my little apartment at the end of the day!

Bears his own destiny - rolled a huge rock - what did he see - poetry alone is truth - i put all my hopes - the absolute you - chooses her repertoire - the facts of the life - this creature in the mirror - a position of weakness.

Did I ride in a cart or walk to Verona? Did the whole town come out to watch? Did Romeo actually live and actually die?

Did I act as Marguerite in London? When I pushed Sarah off the shelf? Or was it Magda? – or Cleopatra? – or some other part?

What if our thoughts are based on imaginings? Are we sitting on clouds or sitting on a stone? What is thinking if our thoughts are as thin as the air?

The young man climbed the ladder.
He was shivering in the cold.

I feel a need to add to my little travelling shrine. My anchor in every bay where I rest my oars. My mother's photograph – my father's broken watch – a letter from my daughter, away at school. Nora's brooch – Hedda's pearls. A chip of paving stone from the streets of Verona. What token, what souvenir, what trophy shall I acquire? My fingers itch – my senses yearn. Something new will soon augment my heart's-display.

What in heaven's name am I going to do with myself?

I cannot bear to face Armand. He is standing right in front of me. I had hoped that I would never meet him again. And yet – I have longed – oh how I have longed – to see that face. Armand is angry – his eyes are ablaze. He insists on telling the world what I am. He throws gold pieces and they bounce off me and fall on the floor. I can only say 'Armand' – only 'Armand'. If only you knew what I am thinking and cannot say.

The husband of the young wife and mother worked in a bank. The husband provided for all life's needs. He made a home for the young mother and her children. In that home the family was safe from the wind and the rain.

Playing small parts in small plays in the early days.
Acting in roles that have nothing to do with me.

Oh – how did I live through those days? What was wrong with me that I lived through those days? – what was right with me that I lived through those days? The words would cut me like a knife. The silences would crush me like a rock. It was a landscape that I struggled out of barely alive.

All the wrong reasons - never again - never again - never again - hide behind a costume - all of life has taken place - the unknown quest - hold our meeting - the only light - a blending of two hearts - bandaged the wounds - sees a scoop.

You have come to interview me. But have you thought about your trade? Does every word open out to a world for you?

All of life is like a play in which one is acting. Here is the furniture – here are the walls – now get out on stage! And the only playwright – aside from God – is the self.

We live the life we don't think about. We imagine the life that we do. Now which of these two lives – if I do decide to talk – would I share with you?

When the florist turned her back,
the boy stole a basket of flowers.

There is no denying the truth. I have reached the end of a road. I am hiding in a hut for a storm to pass by. What will the clearing skies reveal? What new path will be open to me? Off with the cloak of the pilgrim – on with the wings of the self. What is the unknown quest on which I must certainly go?

I set you free from all your obligations.

Climbing up the ladder. Naples – Turin – within sight. Someday Rome? – or Paris? – or St. Petersburg? London, perhaps? – New York? I have no idea how Sarah started out. Was she a rag-tag child of wandering thespians? – sleeping under a wagon and dreaming of stars?

In the evenings,

A writer who only writes while alone.
Cold rain beating against a door.
A huge burden on a shoulder.

the dog would wait

So – any anecdotes from those days?
The days of the travelling troupe of actors?
The days when you were a young actress making your way?

outside the theatre.

Reading a novel by the poet, D'Annunzio! It has set my mind aflame! He has the knack of seeing gold where there is dross! His words are sparks of passion – his pen has left scorches on the page! Ink – to pen – to hand – to heart? Why was he so unprepossessing when I was so unimpressed with him in Rome?

For my fate no tear is shed, no friend makes moan.

I said goodbye to those wretched camellias. I shall never wear them again. Only fresh spring flowers from now until I am gone. I look up and am stunned and surprised! It is Armand! – it is Armand! Oh he must not see me like this! I have wasted away to a stick while he has been gone! He approaches with tears in his eyes! My own begin to flow! Let them flow! – let me sink! – let me die! He gently holds me in his arms! I am loved! – I am loved! – I love Armand!

Chapter 4

A man steps out of a gondola. The break of dawn on the Grand Canal. I am standing at the dock. Restlessness has brought me to this spot. D'Annunzio – the poet. I introduce myself. He says he knows exactly who I am. He is here to give a speech. I have been hoping that we would meet – I almost tell him so, but I manage to bite my tongue. The sun is rising over his shoulder – the golden waters of the canal. Artist to artist – heart to heart. Our eyes speak more than do our words.

He saw himself in the spendour of his own blood.

Finally I have a role. Not a slew of dull words on a page but a living, breathing, heart-and-soul person on the stage. I am now the premiere actress. I have the role at the centre of it all. Every breath that is taken on stage is focused on me. I am a mother and a wife – I have a heart and I have a soul. The other actors are astonished – I can see it in their eyes. They have never seen this dull play come so alive. They have never thought of a play as if it was real. I clutch my success with fingers of steel! I wave the reviews as I make my demands! From now on, I want the lead in every play!

A visit

Two people baring their hearts on a gondola ride.
An audience looking for an actress in a role.
The blinding light of the blade of a knife.

to the region

What is your sense of the depth of this young reporter?
Is he aware that you might have alternative plans?
That there might be hidden motives in your words?

of death.

A touch of colour on a bit of canvas.

An infinitely pleasurable mystery.
The power to abolish all memory.

The poet entered into the court by the south door. He felt contempt for the vain stupidity of the paltry assemblage – an insult to the splendid architecture of former glorious Venetian days. I think of myself as an uncut book – a tabernacle sealed – a useless, action-less ornament, tossed like a sop to this mediocre crowd. To give a speech in which I conceal much more than I say? – at which they will yawn and give a smattering of bored applause? Do they think that this is the summit of my ambition? From the bank of San Giorgio Maggiore, a rocket hissed up in the air and burst into spendour.

She who has forgotten her own face.

Italy is very small. She is a new country with very little in the way of a legitimate stage. The dramatic world belongs to the English and the French. They have the playwrights – they have the plays. They have the theatres – they have the audiences – they have the acclaim. They have all the great roles in the repertoire.

The young girl had a brother who was leaving. Before he left, he gave her sage advice. He was the brother who she expected would always protect her. But he was off to live in another land.

"Duse is the best Electra this critic has ever seen."
"Euripides would know her instantly."

My life has been smashed with a hammer – a myriad of fragments on the parlour floor. I know how painful it is to fit them together again. Nora herself must break the vase. Some pieces will be lost and some will be found. It will be serviceable, but never quite the same.

Feel a close bond - continues on and on - how steep the cliff - refresh and renew - crushed by a cloud - know each other's thoughts - wait for her to live - no one says a word - control the narrative - sudden changes of direction.

Do you think that time is our greatest enemy? Do you think that time is our greatest friend? Ever wonder where the time comes from and where it goes?

Find it difficult to sleep? Read a good book or sew or crochet? Wonder why the clock is so reluctant to move?

What is the brightest star in your heaven? What is the bitterest memory that lies at the bottom of your well? Are you at all introspective – is that what you are?

The washerwoman begged mercy from the monarch.

The king sat in his royal robe and shrugged.

There are yearnings that start in childhood. There are yearnings that start in the womb. There are yearnings that we suck with our ancestry through the cord. I am tired of acting in the Italian language in French plays for French audiences. I am tired of acting in the Italian language in English plays for English audiences. Why couldn't Juliet be written by one of ours?
Both were now face to face with the truth.
A fishing village on the Tuscan coast. My son is born – my son dies. I met his father in Rome – in a hotel room. A rose in his button-hole – a child in me. What are 'we' going to do? – order poison or champagne? The room was accommodating – the father was not. I left and walked the streets as I waited for the train. Never again – never again – never again.

The young lady's father was a powerful Venetian. In the senate he wielded much power. He was against the lady's choice of a husband. He cursed her as she stood by her chosen one's side.

Meeting a poet who wishes to be a dramatist.
Imagining the plays that he could write for me.

"Eleonora Duse presents her characters as living, everyday people whom one could know – which is the last thing one would want to see on the stage. Sarah Bernhardt presents her characters as heroic, romantic, larger than life – the grand gesture and the statuesque pose. All the heightening that suggests the classical, exalted ideal. We can see daily life in our homes, on the streets, in the lobby of the theatre. On the stage we prefer to see those more elevated than the washerwoman or the operator of the tram. Give us something to look up to – give us the glory of the grandest ages – give us the personages who are not as mundane as ourselves. We buy flowers in the marketplace from the likes of La Dusa's portrayals, and hand them up to Sarah on the stage."

The inextinguishable flame - insists on working alone - not his original plan - a jewel in a casket - the composite soul - die rather than share - eat no bread and drink no wine - i doffed my armour - a shop with masks - his unformed self.

What is the loneliest night that you can remember? The night when the clock seemed to be laughing in your face. The night when the dawn held back an hour or two in spite.
Ever spend a night in Venice? A lonely night out on the canal? In a gondola with an old man who just wants to go home?
One by one the lights are extinguished. Everyone safely tucked in their beds. The only light is the one that you left burning in your room.

People looked in awe
as the eagle flew in the sky.

The poet stood and thought in his misery. From the torch in the candelabra, a ruddy glow. How to communicate to the masses? – how to make every word have an action for its aim? How to impress the rhythm of art on the life of a city which has forgotten its innermost self? How to embellish the people's existence – how to make them dream of spendours – how to renew the blood that should animate life with art? To find the metaphors that would move a thousand stuffed-shirts?

The sea sometimes overflowed the dunes.

Sarah Bernhardt is the queen of the dramatic world. She acts in English and in French. She acts in Paris, in London, and in New York. She has been the queen of the stage for many years. She has a fifteen year head-start on me. What Sarah has done – I know that I can do too.

An interview that is not an interview.
A woman whose lover has gone away.
Shallow-good and shallow-bad reviews.

I always act in mime. There is nothing else I can do. France – England – Russia. South America – the United States. I am forced to act in Italian – it is the only language I know. The audience hears words that they cannot understand. Sarah chooses the windmill gesture – she does it all with her hands and her arms. She throws herself all over – on the divan, on the chair, on the floor. I act with my face – I let the story give me my cues. I let the sunlight and the shadows move across my unpainted face. My face is naked – Sarah wears a mask.

I go into a tiny shop.
I have never seen it before.
I have passed this way many times.
I am surprised that I have been so unaware.

Is he one to simply parrot your bland comments?
Would he have no thoughts of his own to add to his blurb?
Would he faithfully, unwarily, serve your greater ends?

It is an ancient Roman coliseum. It has seen its better days. It has sat in the sun for almost two thousand years. A platform has been set up in a tiny corner. People are paying a penny to see a rag-tag play.

Here is the dovecote where the Nurse used to sit.

In the sun against the wall.
Right here is where young Juliet broke her brow.

The secret was very simple. She chose roles which spoke to her heart. She effaced herself completely. She let the characters use her body as a medium. She became every character she played.

We walked what seemed like miles that day. I could have walked hundreds more. So light – so springy – were my steps. Mountains and valleys were nothing to me because you were there. I avoid all mountains now – I avoid all valleys as well. I prefer desert sand between my toes.

To cut off worldly communication.
Two guardian columns of granite.
The bank of the Piazzetta.

There is Shakespeare, Wilde, Shaw – Dumas-fils, Rostand and Sardou. Where are the writers that we can compare? Aeschylus, Sophocles, Euripides – all wrote wonderful parts for me. Surely there is no lack of nutrients in our soil. I want Italy to have her own magnificent body of dramatic works.
Old and string-less musical instruments.
Am I alive? Sometimes I wonder. A child – a wife – a mother. I have a self who stands beside me – watching all these things happen to someone else. Now I am watching myself give birth to a little girl.
She suffered cruelly by the hand she adored.
A daughter is born to me – a daughter is born to me. Oh the days I spent with my mother – oh the days she spent with me. Walking beside the cart on the way to another town. This is my mother come to me – as this child I hold in my arms. I shall call you Enrichetta – I put all my hopes in this name. You are my mother – and you are me – for better or worse.

The lady's father was the source of her opulent life-style. He was a man with a social position of command. Her father died and the lady was left without a penny. Her father's pistols were his only legacy.

"She brings a great love to her art."
"Every atom of Duse's being is at her command."

The oars ply purposefully in the water. Courting Egypt – challenging Rome. My master sees the crown that hides the dagger. My master sees the figs that hide the asp. Better he stumble in his tent and fall on his sword.

What is he thinking - all they are to me - watch my entire life - the best
way out - all toil in similar fields - crutch or splint or bandage - will not slum-

ber - kiss myself awake - brood and brood and brood - not with a knife.

You know, I didn't always want to be an actress. Though I started at four years old. As time went on, I thought I would like to be one of the press.

Seeing life as a gold-fish bowl. With other people than me as the fish. I would look at them through the glass and take the odd note.

I would share these notes with my friends. What they ate and how they dressed. All the trivia that all my friends would want to know.

The young man climbed the ladder.
He was a thinking young man
with brilliant ideas.

The cannon announced the progress of the Queen and a quiver ran through the crowd. The young poet formed a mental picture of the aging actress. She was poisoned by too much living – she was worn by too much art. Her tragic face now bore the marks of a hundred masks. She reached out to him – yes, to help him – to inspire him in his art – but he shuddered at the arid veins in her aging hands. Yet she was needed for inspiration – he had asked her to stand near as he spoke. She was all the inspiration he currently had.

A violent instinct to revolt against fate.

Sarah has conquered in every role. Sarah has conquered in every play. Sarah has conquered every audience. Sarah has conquered every reviewer. Sarah's castles guard the landscape of the legitimate stage.

The young woman's husband treated their home as a doll's house. He loved to treat his wife as another child. The young mother was happy to be treated as one of the children. Only occasionally would she sneak a macaroon.

Acting the lead in challenging plays.
All the lightning in the sky crackles in me.

Oh you must wear this costume.
I have made it from whole cloth.
I have cut it out and sown it as a surprise.
I made it from cloth of my favourite colour.
It is the you that I often see when I close my eyes.

The knack of seeing gold - surrounded by these things - a tabernacle sealed - everyone says - takes on a new sheen - i am marble constant - the bitterest memory - ophelia for sure - sitting on clouds - stumble in his tent.

Who is the biggest trophy in your display case? The biggest celebrity that you have caught? What kinds of questions do you ask them – to catch them off-guard?

Have you ever interviewed Sarah? What is the real Sarah like, do you think? What is the Sarah underneath all the Sarahs we see?

Perhaps you could write a book – a book about Sarah's deepest thoughts. Sarah is such a publicity-seeker. All you would have to do is scribble while Sarah talked.

When the king turned his back,
the boy stole a basket of coins.

I meet with the poet D'Annunzio again. There are only five years between us, so we have like hearts and like minds. He is a little vain about his person, but has little right to be – a slight baldness and pouches under his eyes. But no matter – he will be my hope for the coming dawn. If he can write plays as he writes poems and novels, he shall be the Italian star – be the Ibsen, the Shakespeare, the spokesman that we need. Oh ye gods of art and romance! – make my future one of great riches! – I beg you! – please!

Streaks of rouge on the wrinkled cheeks of an old woman.

First roles – first roles – I am the reason for staging the play. I am the prima-dona of the acting troupe. People come to see la Duse. They are enchanted by my reviews.

A little girl

A novel set in 1883.
A lady who tells her husband the truth.
A victim feeling a knife enter her back.

would play

Do you hope that he sees a scoop in what you tell him?
Do you hope that he sees no greater scoop than this?
That he will act as would a maid in one of your plays?

with the dog.

The young poet reveled in the splendid future which he knew would be his. He would exalt himself and magnify his dreams of beauty and power. His genius for imagery would be his invincible force. He felt his forehead to be illuminated by a ray of light. The poet's eyes caught sight of the aging actress. His heart quickened at the young woman by her side.

Consent to sing the lyric parts of another's tragedy.

I must take the battle to Sarah. She has a hostile army which guards the stage. I must conquer the theatre-world of Sarah's domain. She will be quite a formidable foe. She will cling with a lioness's will to what she has come to see as hers – and hers alone. She will not slumber on the battlements. How shall I take the ramparts of Paris – by stealth or by force?

Chapter 5

The poet has something that he wishes to tell me. He is almost handsome in the glow of the torches along the canal. He wants to make a confession. He leans closer after glancing at the gondolier.

Here's the smell of blood still.

Moving from village to town to city. A string of acting companies – a string of roles. The Lagunaza Company – the Benicasa Troupe – the Ciotti, Belli-Blanes Company – the Fiorentini Company. The most popular plays and playwrights. Sardou – Meilhac – Legouvé – Augier – Pailleron. Marenco – Torelli – Ferrari. My father seeing an opportunity – or I. We take turns leading – we both comply. Each is a rung on a wooden ladder – a gleaming step on a marble staircase. Each is a chance to see a little more of the sky.

The region where

A rivalry between two great actresses.
A river which rises and floods a plain.
A person who makes a rare exception.

the embryos

You are noted for not giving many interviews?
Is that a fair comment for me to make?
That you often turn down what other actresses crave?

blink their eyes.

The palace of the Doges.
A mysterious murmur within a sea-shell.
The divinity of the poetic hour.

He had always planned to meet me. He knew me by reputation and attended one of my plays. He watched me play Marguerite, when I was in Rome.

Why did you not come backstage? I tried, but there was a guard who barred the door.

I say that you will see Agamemnon dead.

Oh, I could never play Lord Hamlet. Sarah has me there. She can hide behind a costume and a make-up mask. But Ophelia and I are generous – me to she and she to I. Ophelia gives me everything I need.

Beware, her brother said, of the male ego. Beware of the male drive. Beware of the crushing hammer of male power. Be sure to always remember who you are.

"Duse's acting is intelligent yet spontaneous."
"Her performances are candid yet still restrained."

Sarah and I on the same stage! This has never happened before! We are playing the same role! She speaks a line and then I speak the same! She strikes a pose and delivers a line in the grandest style! And then I speak my line in the simplest way!

Nothing to do with me - the simple truth - the same old roles - a grain of salt - never see a camellia - hurricanes of despair - an uncut book - clung to the young girl - how can we think - seen its better days.

Are you an artist in your profession? Are you an artist in your life? Do you try to shape your life to an ideal?

When you sit and eat your breakfast? When you walk across the street? Do you think of yourself as fashioning a work of art?

Is there a moment when you dip your brush? What are the colours of the paint in the various cans? If your elbow knocks one over, what do you have?

A vagabond heard news of tomorrow's hanging.
The vagabond sat in his royal robe and shrugged.

I bided my time to see you again, he says. I wrote my poems and I followed your career. You were the great Italian mystery – there was no knowledge of your personal life. You were truly a woman who only lived on the stage.

I have courage enough for it now.

My affair with Cafiero. Something I try not to think about. He so handsome – dashing – sophisticated. Me – Eleonora – so naive. He leaving me with a broken heart and an unborn child – the boy who was never born. I will carry him, always, inside me. All the love I withhold from others I will keep for this child.

The young lady and her husband took separate ships to Cyprus. A great storm threatened to sink the ships at sea. Each braved the angry ocean and landed safely. Their happiness was at its height that day.

Riding in a gondola at dawn on the Grand Canal.
A blending of two hearts and two minds.

In the audience are all the reviewers from all the cities that we have played! Reviewers to whom Sarah has given countless interviews! Reviewers whose invitations I have always refused! I recognize the theatre! The gilded boxes! – the chandeliers! Sarah has invited me to act on her personal stage!

All of my truths - has no conception - blood in the waves - enchanted by my reviews - we regret the loss - reached down into the mud - walk around inside this skull - felt an imperious demand - don't suit my talent - remove the honey.

Do you ever wonder what life was like on the very first day? Imagine the end of that first day on earth. The light was fading over the mountains – the people stood at the mouth of the cave – each one wondered whether the light would ever return.

Why did they make those drawings that we see on the walls of the caves? Those drawings were put there, I assume, at the end of that very first day. And why do the images get darker as we carry our fading torch deeper and deeper into the bowels of the cave?

And when they looked at those paintings, what did each of them think they were seeing? The beast they had caught – and on which they had feasted – or the beast that got away? And who was alive because they had caught the beast, and who was dead for the same reason? – or who was alive and who was dead because the beast got away?

As they walked
they trod the star underfoot.

To me, you are the embodiment of the present and the past. You are the actress who makes the classics come alive. What is the secret, if I might ask? I have had some success as a poet – as a novelist of some note – but I could never hope to write as well as you act. The night is cold and there is only one blanket to share.

These are laws by which I would not wish to live.

I sit and watch a play – as Ophelia. She sits and watches a play – as me. Beside us sits Lord Hamlet. He of the letters whose pages have burned my hands. He of the letters whose words have burned my eyes.

Two adjacent empty villas above a town.
Facts that are meager and sparse.
The necessary fuel for life and art.

I know nothing of technique. Sarah's technique is mechanical. She counts to five every night before she replies to Armand. I sat and counted when I watched her in the theatre. I tell people I have no technique. I see these women in me – I see myself in these women. Let Sarah count to five before she speaks. Each performance is new to me. I find myself speaking different words to Armand.

A man emerges from behind a curtain.
I have been waiting for you, he says.
I have been waiting for you for centuries.
I serve all the carnival guests.

Have you had some bad luck in your dealings with the press?
Is that why you so seldom agree to talk?
Would you care to explain why privacy is so important to you?

I am fourteen, I say to myself. I am Juliet and I am fourteen years old. I have a basket of roses in my hand. I am standing on my balcony looking down. I am fourteen now and shall be fourteen for the rest of my life.

There's something special about Verona.
I wouldn't want to be anywhere else.
It is a town where all of life has taken place.

She was a diva in her prime. She put herself in service to every drama. Every role was the essence of that character. She portrayed their naked compulsions, griefs and joys. While on-stage she – herself – would cease to exist.

There is not one thing that I owe you. I paid every bill at the highest price. I paid for every brilliant moment of our time together. The cost of that smile – of those words, of those dreams, of those promises – has been far in excess of the pleasure that they gave.

Youthful royalty and beauty.
Forgetting one's prosaic existence.
The gift of eternal poetry.
The storied walls and waters.

I tell him my personal life is nondescript. It has no bearing at all. I give everything I have to my art – to the stage. When I am not on stage I do not exist, I say.

Is Antony or we in fault for this?

Who will you be, Enrichetta? – you who lie here in my arms. A snuggling kitten – a suckling puppy at my breast. You can be anyone but me. The years ahead will tell us who you choose to be.

Why do I weep for this so piteously?

I buy my daughter a puppet. The arms move – the legs move. The mouth moves up and down. She will be able to make it walk and make it talk. And when she flings it into a corner, it will stay for days and days. The two of them will give each other life.

The lady was aging and limited in prospects. A marriage of convenience was the only path she could see. A dull drudge asked her to marry him and she accepted. He promised her horses and the hosting of fancy-dress balls.

"Duse projects the feelings of her characters with grace and power."
"A level of acting that other actors cannot achieve."

Am I Sarah? – is she me? Am I not-Sarah? – is Sarah not-me? We are drawn together by each of us speaking the same lines! The lines that Dumas-fils has written for us to say! We are kept apart by the way we speak our lines! How can two people be so different? – so the same?

The less she knows - a drop of poison - from head to foot - these agonizing thoughts - not shed a tear - alone – alone – alone - help the situation - making my way - the voice within myself - clutching the truth.

They didn't have answers – they had questions. They had questions expressed in art. A smear of paint from a natural source – daubed on a wall.

Well, this is not a popular subject, I'm sure. Art as the torch that illuminates life. All of life was there – do you see? – on that very first day.

It's what you find in all the great plays. It's what you find if you open your eyes. Not what you find in the newspapers that are hawked on the streets.

The young man climbed the ladder.
To keep himself warm
he planned to burn each rung below.

But you are a poet who is gaining in national prominence. I have read some of your poems – and one of your novels as well. You are imaginative in the extreme. I would much rather hear a little bit more about you.

It is such a narrow-minded way of looking at things.

What in these actors and their actions does Lord Hamlet see? He mutters comments as the actors ply their trade. He could be a drama critic, so acute are his perceptions. I'll admit that the play seems Greek to me.

One day the young woman's husband developed an illness. She was happy to play the nurse and look after his health. But it turned out that he needed an operation. It was an operation that the family could ill afford.

Mouldering in a tiny room in a fishing village.
An unborn child who suckles at my breast.

The oar flashed in the water. They were afloat on the Grand Canal. It was a beautiful evening at festival time. Each was uncertain of the other. There was trouble in their minds. Each of them had a sense that something was terribly wrong. He was pale and thoughtful – was she the one to complete him? – perhaps she lacked the gravity to inspire. She looked at her lover with a fleeting smile – was he the one to complete her? – she felt that he was in need of perpetual praise. Was she the compliment to his vision? – was he the compliment to hers? Imperfect love – imperfect love – imperfect life.

The sap refuses to flow - nurse that dream - illuminated by a ray of light - awaiting its fatal cue - trapped in a store-room - cranked out like sausages - the life-boat springs a leak - the river, the bridge, the shops - who have paid the bills - doling out the rations.

Perhaps you are an artist – whether you know it or not. You put ideas into peoples' minds. Your readers laugh and cry at your command.
People rely on you for sustenance. Your words are their meat and their drink. You can light a candle for them or blow one out.

Oh, you sit there nodding your head! You make me nervous! – you make me sad! Perhaps I should throw myself off the balcony! – or I should throw you!

When the executioner turned his back,
the boy's head was in a basket
on the ground.

I have confessed that I wanted to meet you. I had hopes that you might inspire me to write a play. His eyes sparkle with inner-vision – he is a man of exciting ideas. We share a candlelight dinner in a small café.
This is the very painting of your fear.
Sarah comes to town! – to Turin, believe it or not! She doesn't know me and doesn't want to – a provincial actress in a small Italian town. Her troupe takes over the theatre – the great lady on our stage! Her cast is medio-

cre, but she doesn't seem to mind. She is the only actor in the play. I attend every performance – I am enthralled. Not by what Sarah does when on stage – but by what she has caused to be true in her life. That she has her own troupe – that she chooses her repertoire. That she could demand better acting – that she could act instead of perform. That she has the power to live on stage should she choose to do so. I have no desire to be Sarah – but I want what Sarah has. I want to command the resources that idly lie in her hands.

She would throw a stick

Two lovers who touch eyes.
Wine in the moonlight at midnight.
Restaging a battle that has been won.

and the dog

Is this what might be called something of a paradox?
That, as an actress, your work is performed in public?
And yet you insist on keeping your private life to yourself?

would bring it back.

The gondola glides to the dock. We have finished our gondola ride. The night is not so young, but there is plenty left to say. I sense that now is not the time to end our talk. This is the entrance to my apartment. Would you like to come inside? I don't often entertain visitors, but I'm sure I can manage to offer a glass of wine.
 The fearful pangs of present vision grow on me.
 I sit beside Lord Hamlet and watch the play. Nearby, as fellow-watchers, sit King and Queen. I see myself in every character. Those who are masters – those who are slaves. Those who are wise and those who are foolish. Those who are doomed and those who will ultimately survive. Does every other watcher see the same?

Chapter 6

Our souls touched last night. We didn't touch hands. We didn't touch lips. We merely touched eyes. We share the same hopes, the same dreams, the same ideals. We want the same things for art, for the drama, for Italy. We formed a partnership – he to write – me to act. To resuscitate and revive – to engender and renew – to revivify and redeem. We shall bring life to the dormant dreams that repose in our souls.

The prisoner is called Radiana.

Taking on more of Sarah's roles. These are the parts that people want to see. Disappointing some of them – where was Sarah in that role? Telling a young reporter that I am a new kind of actress. I act each part as I feel it – I am not playing a role. I do not wave my arms and burst into tears. I ask the audience to watch my face as closely as they can. Clouds and sunshine move across it in wave after wave. You are not sitting in the audience at a loud and raucous play. Hearts are breaking with the quietest of words. Think and feel as if you are living on the stage.

The region where

A poet writing a novel and a play.
A mask which chooses a face.
A mirror that never gives advice.

the skeletons

Why so many topics in this talk that you are having?
Are you preparing, perhaps, a journalistic Trojan Horse?
What is the ultimate objective of your plans?

flinch on the brink of death.

All the forces of human life.
Desires of a feverish intensity.

An irresistible temptress.

The poet ascended the marble steps of the platform. The crowd, to him was a thousand-faced monster. The seething hall was like a many-eyed chimera – its scales gave off light like sparkling jewels. The beast was devoid of all thought as it waited to hear his words. In all the gathering, he alone was expected to think. His eyes sought the tragic actress in the front row.

I do not wish to be loved thus.

Arriving in Paris to play Marguerite. Sarah has made a big splash in the newspapers. Welcoming the new young apprentice-actress to Sarah's town. She offers me the use of her personal theatre. A star and a lock on her dressing-room door. The janitor takes me out into the alley and down a few doors. Sarah's dressmaker mutters and scolds – are you playing a waif or a drab? Sarah's jeweler throws up his hands – are you playing Marguerite or her lowly Italian maid?

The young girl then turned to her father. A man who always gave her sage advice. He told her to always be wary of others' motives. The last thing you should do is relax your guard.

"The actors who surround her are so mediocre."
"Duse is a wave of poetry amidst a sea of dull prose."

"Duse, with her unfailing hold and yet exquisitely delicate touch upon her part in the play, her sleeplessly vigilant sense of beauty of thought, feeling and action, and her prodigious industry, must be recognized as a supreme athlete of the stage, compared with whom the ranters are weaklings and sluggards. When Duse gives us her best work, we cannot be too emphatic in declaring that it is the best of the best and magnificent; so that our hall-mark may be carried through the nations on a piece of sterling gold."

No tear is shed - sitting on a stone - my own ledger - words have burned my eyes - just the thought of it - the bottom of your well - take turns leading - hiding in a hut - a rag-tag child - marks of a hundred masks.

Tell me about yourself. Tell me all about yourself. No – you don't want to, do you?

Why do you hesitate? Are there things you don't want me to know? Are there secrets for which you would die rather than share?

Are you married? Do you have a wife? A child perhaps? – a daughter?

*The eagle doffed its mighty wings
and hung them on a rack.*

Yes, we all take sustenance from other human beings. They are the fruit that hangs from the trees. They are the vegetables that lie in the fields. I feed my love and he feeds me. Oh I was a fool for many years. I thought I could only be alive while on a stage.

A dazzling meteor obscuring the light of the stars.

Checchi offers to take me on. He is lonely and I am alone. Not the same, but similar enough. He is decent, frugal, faithful – all the things the world is not. A weak moment, perhaps, for me – perhaps not. Money – health – companionship – the having and the have-not. He offers to be the floor on which I can stand. He will dedicate himself to me – I will dedicate myself to my art. Bargains like these have led to heaven – have led to hell.

There were celebrations on the island of Cyprus. Bonfires were lit and everyone on the island shouted with joy. It seemed as if the island was a peaceful haven. The Turkish fleet had been broken by the storm.

Forming a pact between two souls.
A pact with locks and bolts as strong as steel.

Oh my sister takes life too seriously. Since when have the gods actually spoken? Far above is far away. Creon and his guards are here and now. Our brother left behind no burial plans.

Branded her a liar - what that is comparable - not an interview - offers to be the floor - eyes filled with confidence - that which we have - lacked the gravity - just being you - all the infamy - what has been done to me.

Tell me all about your relationships – how you think and how you feel. How all these people treat you – how you treat them. How often you laugh with them – how often you cry.

Tell me all about your childhood. Tell me how often you skinned your knee. Who were your parents and did you start working at four years old?

What did your parents do for you – what did you do for them in return? Are they alive, still, and happy? What do these old, white-haired people mean to you?

The handsome peasant
approached the puddle.

The young poet's eyes found the eyes of the tragic actress. Near the railing that encircled the celestial sphere. He drank the adoration that he found there – his voice took on the rhythm of the oars. He spoke of a dream of infinite beauty – presented the magic of his words. Told the assemblage that poetry alone is truth – that they should see themselves as swollen by the weight of an unborn world. The crowd leaned forward in rapt wonder – in his hand, he felt, he held their blended souls.

The most secret depths of the will.

Acting on Sarah's stage. In Sarah's role – in Sarah's Paris – in front of Sarah's audience – with Sarah's reviewers taking notes. Unable to concentrate on my role – to be myself as Marguerite. I know every mechanical move that Sarah makes. Though I wear none, I hear the rattle of Sarah's jewelry. I am nervous – my eyes are blurry – I play the part in a nowhere land – neither the Marguerite of Sarah nor of myself. I break my concentration – I glance out at Sarah's box as Armand speaks. I see Sarah bathed in light – she revels in my attention. She is welcoming me to her lair – playing her magnanimous, Sarah-the-Grand-Dame role. All eyes are turned on Sarah – none on me.

A poet known as 'the master of the flame'.
Two people butting their heads against a wall.
An actress who is the essence of Antiquity.

My retreat – my hotel room – my personal cave. A cove along the coastline – a quiet bay. All the stresses and the agonies of a tour. My little shrine on an antique table. The photograph of me and my mother has pride of place. I have been wind-blown – I have been tossed. I have been drifting, in heaving seas, towards the rocks. On this table is the anchor of my thoughts. Without my anchor, I would sink beneath the waves.

The mask-master takes me by surprise.
Here, slip this on, he says.
The mask clings to my face.
It seems to melt into my skin.

Is he, perhaps, playing a game that you are not aware of?
Is his game to let you put yourself off-guard?
To let you hang yourself with rope of your own choosing?

Every word I speak is magical. Every word is a gift to me. I speak at the speed of Shakespeare's pen as it moves across the page. Somehow he knows that it is me who is bringing these words alive. Out of all the Juliet-Sarahs ranged in a row.

This is where Mercutio gave his speech.
The speech about Queen Mab.
If you listen, you can almost hear him speak.

She sought to make her audience feel more deeply. She raised them to a higher level of thought. None of their thoughts was merely for just the moment. Their tears were for the agonies of the world. She was an actress who aroused their hopes and their fears.

Love is a shallow well. A shallow wishing-well. And I fell in. For many days, for many months, I looked up at the sky. My feet in brackish water. And then – I climbed back out, slimy stone by slimy stone.

The desire to concentrate one's thoughts.
A vehement and passionate soul.
A mingling of love and terror.

A single torch burned at the dock. The sun was about to come up. It was clear to me that someone was expected to arrive. The air was cool – the breeze was brisk – the day was about to dawn no matter what. I'll just stand here for a while, I thought to myself.

I cannot believe the energy that he is releasing in me. Until now, I was working strictly on my own. I have had partners in the theatre many times before, but never a creative partner. Not a partner who shares my mind – who shares my soul. They were the ones to handle the money and pay the bills. He is the one to write the words that I shall say. We will do great things together, he and I.

Their trunks were already budding anew.

Facing death and staring it down. Face to face and telling death that I will not die. Come back when I have done what I feel I must do. Sending Enrichetta away – I cannot be a mother to her. I will not drag her around as I was dragged around. She will have the life that I have never had. Food and a table for every meal. A roof overhead for every rainstorm. A tablecloth and knives and forks and spoons. Better than me – that is what she will be. She will lead the life that I have never had.

A judge had his eye on the situation. He knew all the mores of the town. He knew what would be accepted and what would be frowned on. He longed to catch the lady in his claws.

"She is a lioness when cornered in the third act."
"Duse glares – she foams at the mouth – she is sublime."

"But when Madame Bernhardt gives us pinchbeck plays and acting that is poor in thought and eked out with odds and ends stripped from her old parts; when she rants at us and brings down the house in a London theatre just as she brings it down in a provincial American one, we must tell her that she can do better than that, and that we will have nothing less than her best. When Madame Bernhardt offers us her reputation instead of first-rate acting, we must reply that we give reputations instead of taking them, and that we accept nothing in exchange except first-rate acting down on the counter, without a moment's credit."

Only a line or two - retained her secrets - where to look - having no thoughts - the shallow roots of desert blooms - could not breathe life - miserable and cold - searching for the roles - not the same - don't envy anyone.

What are your deepest, most powerful yearnings? What are your cruelest, tear-stained regrets? What is the moment that you would snatch back if only you could?

Any great loves in your life? Did the biggest fish get away? Did you feel as if it was you who swallowed the hook?

Tear open your chest and expose your heart. Let everyone see its feeble beat. Let everyone in the world have a front-row seat as you meekly expire.

Every night
he would write a sonnet
to his mistress.

The young poet spoke with the voice of an angel – the blood was rioting through his veins. The hearts of the people and the voice of the poet pulsed as one. The cold museum regained its spirit – the ancient walls their former life. The poet floated above the crowd. Venice was once more the queen of the sea. He gave the people their centuries of former glory – taught them to see with different eyes – he taught them to dream of a future Venice with different souls.

Remembrance of you aided me in evoking her.

A stack of newspapers on the table. I ask my friends to leave me alone. I struggle through waves of ink in my faulty French. 'La Duse has no conception of the role of Marguerite.' 'The Italian actress was nervous and definitely not in diva-form.' 'She should take notes while watching Sarah in the role.' 'Madame Sarah has triumphed gloriously over La Duse.' I call the maid and point to the papers and point to the fire.

Where would the young wife get the money to save her husband? It was needed to pay the huge medical bill. As a woman, she had no access to money. All she knew was that she should save her husband's life.

Challenging Sarah in her den.
Crawling back home to lick my wounds.

My skull is – sometimes – like an echo chamber. The words that cannot be unspoken bounce down the canyon from rock to rock. What I said to him – what he said to me. What I should have said instead – what I wished he would say that he never said. A journey through a valley of mis-spoken words.

Leave me broken here - read the other's reviews - a many-eyed chimera - has been far in excess - there are yearnings - a facer of facts - find a better place - that ideal world - the night is cold - put the past behind.

Do you enjoy being peppered with questions? Do you squirm in the spot-light's barrage? Is every pimple and mole and scar now on display?

How does it feel to be a celebrity? To have your most precious secrets spread out on display? To have your whole life splattered in ink across a page?

No – you wouldn't want that would you? No – you wouldn't want to be me. All you want is to sit and scribble while I bleed.

She owned the sun; he owned the moon.
He depended on her light.

He says he wants to make love to me when I come off the stage. In the dressing room or first thing in the hotel. Drenched in the sweat of Medea, Electra, Cassandra. I am not jealous, for they are all me. I am Medea, Electra, Cassandra in flesh and bone. I tell him this and he tells me – we agree in every word. I am his slave-girl – I am his queen. I am his living, breathing – throbbing – present-in-the-past.

An invincible force hastened him through life.

A young Italian reviewer on the train. He overheard Sarah saying that I do not act. 'A peasant who wanders onto the stage!' 'A Marguerite without any jewelry? – what a skin-flint is Duse's Armand!' Would I care to make a comment for the Italian press?

The girl would hold

A flock of children on ancient streets.
Writing words by candlelight.
Two actresses performing in the same role.

a piece of bread

Is this a duet? – is it a duel?
Is it a game of deadly chess?
Will there be blood on the floor when the final curtain descends?

and the dog would eat.

He gave them the garden of their rich inheritance – grafted the present onto the past. In the works of the painters and sculptors – in those who paint and sculpt in words – life reveals itself as rich in all good things. The poet tamed the dreaded chimera – pressed out the essence of life itself. Voiced the unspeakable, ceaseless longings – the secret of inexpressible dreams. Youthful hearts beat faster at the breath of the poet's words. From the open door of the balcony, a fresh breeze wafted in from the ancient lagoon.

The taste of worldly corruptness on those eloquent lips.

All the dreams of ancient Venice – cradled in her infancy, in art on the ceilings and the walls; buried, stifled for centuries – now came alive. Now embodied – alive and breathing – in this poet who stood before them. In his person they saw the inextinguishable flame. There was silence in the room – on every lip was the taste of fine wine. The young poet's eyes found the tragic actress – but what was she looking at? Her eyes were smiling at someone in the distance – a young and beautiful woman – an image, it seemed, of his own inexpressible thought.

His delirium swelled the muscles of the gods.

On the train on my way back to Italy. My friends search hard for a few kind words to pass on to me. Sarah has praised – they say – my acting in all the Paris newspapers. For once, her critics say that Sarah is wrong. 'Madame Sarah's only fault is her magnanimous generosity.' 'There is no actress like our Sarah – she is Marguerite as no one else could ever be.' 'The Paris audiences know her every pose – every gesture is always applauded whenever she plays.' 'And as for the little Italian – she has completely and utterly failed.' 'Sarah has routed her impertinent rival from the stage'.

Chapter 7

We are in love and we are creative. We are the embodiment of our age. From we two, thousands of people will take their cue. They will look to us for leadership – a new kind of play – a new kind of stage. A new kind of woman who is not a statue or a drab. We are a couple who know what a relationship should be. My love is eager to dip his pen and fill the page.

You are naught, you are naught; I'll mark the play.

Le Monde Ou L'On S'Amuse – Le Gelosie di Lindoro – La Princesse de Bagdad. I breathe life into these plays. I find the thread of emotion that ties me to every character on the stage. I make these actors become these people. I do it with my voice and with my eyes. Do not act in a play with me while thinking of your laundry-bill or where you are going to dine after the show. You are a person whose heart is beating every minute of your life. Every other person on stage takes life from that heart. Not for one minute are you to be a mechanical doll.

Life and death

An actress playing a character in a play.
The label on a bottle of printers' ink.
A brother giving advice to his sister.

at every moment

Now – is this a delicate topic?
Perhaps you will stop me before I begin?
Do you mind if I ask some personal questions of you?

in every play.

The end of a deserted canal.
Floating on dead waters.
A brain that seems on fire.

There are so many glorious topics. All of history is our source. Everyone who has ever been alive has had a heart that beats as mine. I want to breathe life into their stories – I want to show them alive on the stage. My love is a brilliant writer – his poems sing – his novels inspire. Now he is turning his hand to drama. I believe – oh how I believe. He has the swagger, the elan, the purpose-fullness. When he sets his mind, there is nothing he cannot do.

I had danced myself tired, my dear judge.

Some day, I would like to play Phedre in French. I tried an interview in that language – once and only once – with a French interviewer. I found I could not find the words. He took my pauses and made an interview out of that. I am Phedre – I am Duse – I am Italian – I am not French. Sometimes it takes me the whole day to become myself.

Her father was an important man in the palace. His role was to do the bidding of the king. The king was suspicious of the motives of the prince. Her father asked the girl to act as a spy.

"Falsehood, guilt, crime, alarm, terror, disgust, hatred."
"Duse does it all with a turn of the head and a flick of the eye."

The remnants of the banquet! Laughter rang so long ago! The perfection of the painting! I sat so still while in my prime! The windows all have shutters! There are locks that bar the door!

Feel a slight twinge - stunned and surprised - impending dramatic struggle - we all take sustenance - we are kept apart - my sense of privacy - my unpainted face - took on the rhythm - think they were seeing - a hostile army.

Put that notebook away and I will tell you something. Listen to me! – listen to me! – as a person who is not a writer! I will pounce on you if you write another word!

Oh don't you see what has happened? The great rock on which I built my reputation has sunk beneath the waves. Gossip has made that rock invisible to the public eye.

He wanted me to be the oil which would light his flame – not only the oil, but the match as well. He was an empty vessel on a table in a darkened room. What could such a cipher write that would be worthwhile?

A peacock took the eagle's wings
and strapped them on his back.

D'Annunzio – D'Annunzio. How I love to murmur that name. He is the other half of my soul. I am the actress – he is the writer. I am the voice – he is the pen. We are the bells in the highest tower. Together we shall make all Italy ring. He has a thousand parts in mind for me. I shall tour them through the world. Every nation shall crave Italian classical plays.

I myself have given myself the cause.

About Ando I have no thoughts. Does a person who fills a void have any presence? When one considers that the void lingers on? I welcome Ando into the void as if it is a cramped phone-booth. There is barely room for me to turn around. The phone is left dangling as I turn and leave the booth.

The young woman's husband pledged eternal fealty. But he was unaware of the forces at work on his mind. A person near to him was watching to undermine his marriage. Sometimes our friends are the ones with the sharpest knives.

Fusing life and art and culture.
Fusing the past the present and the future.

I call the servants to the entrance! The faithful hands that bring me food! I have decided to reverse my orders! I no longer wish to be confined! Remove the nails from the windows! – remove the locks from the door! Bring me a mirror that I might see what I have become!

I was mutilated - much battered and bruised - sensed a secret soul - she depends on others - the same old roles - control the entire play - carcasses on the beach - manage to bite my tongue - we are the thoroughbred - no matter where I go.

He didn't want a Duse. He thought he wanted a Duse, but he had no conception of a Duse. He had me right in front of him and didn't see what you and I can see.

He wanted a Bernhardt – not a Duse. He wanted a Sarah – with all the flash and fireworks and spectacle. He wanted the bubbles on the surface of the stream.

And finally, he realized his dream. He took his play to Sarah – his proper muse. A shallow character in a very shallow play.

It was a true meeting of souls – he and Bernhardt. Two shallow souls with the shallow roots of desert blooms. I was well rid of him as he was well rid of me.

The Queen
lay down her robe.

I stand at the open window. The breeze is fresh and cool. I tell him of the roles I should like to play. A blending of Ibsen and Shakespeare. I tell him I don't like Dumas and Sardou. *La Dame aux Camellias* is a tired old workhorse. She is Sarah's kind of play. I am an actress – not a costume. I don't wear makeup – I don't wear wigs. Let's show the humanity in these women of yesteryear.

You have touched on my bitterest thought.

Oh I am Phedre and I am bleeding. I am wounded – oh how I am wounded. I took off my armour in the midst of the field of battle. The smoke of the cannons – the reek of the dead. The fires on which the bodies had all been piled. I thought the battle had been won. I thought the captain was my ally. I doffed my armour and then he stealthily reached for his sword. I could feel the cold of the steel as it sought my heart.

A person who has paid every bill.
A performance compared to sterling gold.
A person who envies no one in the world.

I wear no makeup – I keep no secrets – I wear no mask upon my face. I am every female who has ever drawn a breath – every female who will ever draw a breath in joy or in pain. The only part I could never play is the part of Sarah, should a play ever be written about her life. Sarah is all performance – Sarah is all for show – she is the puppeteer inside the mechanical doll.

I laugh and I explain.
I would rather choose my own.
I raise my hands and grasp the mask.
But the mask is stuck to my face.

A few questions, if I may ask, about your family?
I mean the family that you acquired of your own?
After your mother and your father passed away?

Every word is warmed by my blood. It ebbs and flows as my heart-beat rises and falls. Juliet-Duse – Duse-Juliet. I am in a state of grace. Me on the balcony – and my Romeo down below.

This is the location of the Friar's cell.
You recall the potion he made.
Juliet was only too eager to drink it down.

She never plastered her face with youthful makeup. She let all her natural flaws and wrinkles show. All her acting was in her voice and in her expressions. She could break a heart with the tremor of her lip. Every thought and every emotion was there to see. People felt that they had met her on the street.

Love, to me, was a lightning-rod. It caught the secrets of the heavens. I climbed a tower on a high hill. I exposed myself to the wind and the rain. I clung to it, fiercely, long after the storm had passed.

The flame and power within oneself.
Poetic imagery and impetuous music.
Some magic fecundation.

My love and I share a single goal. He tells me of his dreams – they are an echo of my own. To dive deep down into the core of one's own self and one's own people. To grasp the pearl that lies on the ocean floor. To present that pearl as a work of imperishable art. Yes! – yes! That is what I have been yearning for! – what has inspired me all of my life! That is what I want to do with you! Together we shall dive from the highest cliff!
What ally should I invoke?
I do not have time for family. I am married to my career. My family is all the roles I play on stage. What am I to do with a daughter? Oh I love you, Enrichetta, but I am the curse that attended your birth. A convent education – a man who will treat you with respect – a quiet life, far away from the life of the stage. Far from the thunderbolts that rain on me from the air.

The lady found her husband disappointing. His promises of luxury disappeared. There was to be no stable of horses. She was not to be the hostess of fancy-dress balls.

"A shudder ran though my body – I was too paralyzed to applaud."
"The old doorman, who has seen them all, said, 'She is the one!' "

A quiet voice then whispers! This is not for us to do! You have warned of this day, my mistress! – every servant took a vow! We must never remove the shutters! – we must never unbar the door! Our mistress's orders must be followed! The orders that you gave while in your prime!

To twist the knife - it was fatal - scurrilous scrap of gossip - came down from the heavens - have a dramatic ending - pour my heart out - completely drained - their own bare eyes - poison or champagne - only i can play.

What he and Sarah didn't know would fill a dozen volumes. The poor play, for the great actress, is not a poor play. The great play, for the poor actress, is not a great play.
You can glide through Venice looking at only the roofs and the spires. And you can consider the man who dredges out the canals. You can laze all day on the bridge and think nothing at all.

All of life is all inside you. From your fingertips to your toes. Not in the hat that you hang on the peg or the socks in the drawer.

Every poem
had the lilt
of a faery song.

We shall build an Italian theatre. It shall be more grand than the theatre at Bayreuth. All of Europe shall come to the opening nights of our plays. Kings and Queens will come to pay homage. The plays will shine like beacons in the dark. Every actress will stand in line to play these parts. This is the dawning of a whole new era – a whole new life.

A little water clears us of this deed.

Oh I am Phedre – miserable and cold. What is a palace when I am locked in the cell of my skull? But I shall not be so confined. I shall become a raging tyrant. I shall brandish a sword of revenge. I shall become the lashing waves of a raging sea. I shall torment myself no more. I shall have my pleasing revenge. His horses shall rear and plunge and twist at the edge of the sea.

The young wife borrowed money from a man who worked with her husband. She knew nothing of the world of finance. She knew nothing of what was legal and what was not. Her only concern was to save her husband's life.

Becoming the people I play on stage.
Taking a knife and severing family from career.

Oh you must look in this mirror.
It distorts both height and size.
Not the you that you are used to.
But the you that others see.
Every feature is an element of your mind.

All is vain - caught the sunlight - the speed of shakespeare's pen - the contents of the book - concentrated her thought - restaging the battle - by implication, in his fiction - life as a gold-fish bowl - adjusted many plays - a position of strength.

Well, I don't think you are learning much in what you had hoped would be an interview. So far, I haven't told you a thing. I've kept all of my true thoughts and all my feelings hidden – in a gold locket – in a chest – buried deep in the back of my mind – in an unlit cave.

Beware the glint – beware the glitter. Beware the bright and shining light. Jewelry shines, but the blinding light is that of the knife.

Oh those eyes! What is behind those eyes? You sit! – you listen! –

your fingers itch to write it all down! But do you think? – is what I am telling you lighting caverns in the dark?

She owned the sun; he owned the moon.
In her presence, he was light.

He is so inspired that he is writing a novel. All about me – all about me – all about me. The shape is gradually forming in his mind. It will have a creative muse – two muses in fact. An older and a younger muse. The older muse will represent the past – a relic, discarded, despised. One who gave him a mild boost in his younger days. A muse of the early jottings of his unformed self – yielding a few thin books of adolescent verse. And I will shine like a radiant angel – I will be the creative muse of his greater years.

Young children, like forms in a dream.

Reading the newspapers as I travel. News of Sarah in every town. How many shoes Sarah owns. How many dresses she has in her closet. How many jewels and how much they cost and the names of the counts and dukes and earls who have paid the bills. Always a fashion-plate on stage – wigs and dresses and makeup and jewelry. Only a line or two about the parts she plays.

The stage-door opened

A collection of gems on a small table.
A singer who reveals the hidden music.
A lady who sits for hours and broods.

and a hand

You have a husband, I believe?
Or perhaps I should say 'had'?
And a daughter who does not, I believe, live with you?

tossed a piece of meat.

But the plays must come first – yes, I insist that the plays come first. Let the new novel bide its time. I realize that you have a need to clear away your past. But – the present is what we have now and is all we need. Settle old scores if you must, but please – please – write the plays before you trifle with other things. I will hold the pens as you write – rub your temples and massage your feet. I will do anything to contribute to our great enterprise.

And in his grave rained many a tear.

Oh I am Phedre – cold and miserable – miserable and cold. I await the news of my actions. I was the sea below the high cliff. I was raging and dealt a horrible blow. Now I wonder what my actions have caused to pass. I wait in a rage of anger and strength – I wait in a stupor of guilt and shame. When am I Phedre? – when am I not? How soon am I to know? I shall know as soon as the news is brought to me.

Chapter 8

Buckling down to work. He insists on working alone. He has always worked alone and he continues with that routine. He has me in his heart – he has me in his mind – he has me as he sees me in his dreams. Besides, I am only a villa away. He can pull on his boots at any time and walk the sacred path, and sneak in my bedroom window and kiss me awake. Many a night he visits my villa – he gets restless when the words fail to come – then, refreshed, he walks back to his cell again.

A person possessed by an incurable madness.

Using my power for my own benefit. Reading every classical play I can get my hands on. Talking to some of the older actresses. What are the great roles? What is the role that you most cherish? What is the role you would have liked to play? Oh to sweep these popular plays from the stage and play nothing but the most challenging female parts in the repertoire. Using my power to bring more classics to the stage.

Two tiny points

A journalist with a notebook on his knee.
A clock that seems reluctant to move.
An actress who brings the past alive.

of competing

What if the young reporter takes his notes to someone else?
Suppose he reads them to the writer of the scabrous book?
Suppose the two of them compose another scurrilous squib?

light.

A flood of inspiration.
All things glowing with a golden light.
A kind of intellectual ecstasy.

The young poet was alone with his thoughts – alone in one of the rooms of the neighbouring museum. He felt the need to quiet his nerves – to get away from contact with the crowd. All of the essence of his spirit had been dissipated, he felt, in the composite soul of the throng. Where to look for renewal of his spirit and his gift? He had sought the eyes of the aging actress, but she had turned away her head. She had looked at the youthful creature of music – who seemed to hold in her hand the flower of flame.

A desire to surpass one's own destiny.

Sarah, on stage, in London, at Daly's theatre. Marguerite in *La Dame aux Camellias*. A French lady speaking in French. Sparkling jewelry, gorgeous dresses, elegant coiffure. Every line is the same each evening. I have seen her perform many times. Night after night every gesture is the same. She counts to five before she speaks to Armand. It is the battle of the divas – the battle of acting styles. The battle of the old and the new. Marguerite is a costume on a hook on the dressing-room door. Every character is Sarah on the stage.

The girl met the prince in a room in the palace. Her father hid and listened to their talk. She had been told that this would help the situation. It was a way that she could act in aid of the prince.

"The audience has bowed before her greatness."
"Duse has made them open their eyes and sit up in their seats."

A pistol shot at the Tesmans'– I'm sure that it was – just a moment ago. I have heard that Hedda practices in the yard. She must have her father's pistol. Tesman himself would never touch one. Now why would Hedda Gabler need a gun?

We are the embodiment - to look at your mind - the splendour of innocent youth - see with different eyes - a state of grace - something of a paradox - naked on the street - sparkle with inner-vision - never a creative partner - paralyzed by the character.

Go your ways! – no, go your ways! I have nothing I care to say! I will not give an interview today!

Were you in London in '95? Were you in New York when I was there? Have you seen my Phedre? – my Marguerite Gautier? – my Hedda Gabler?

Have you seen Bernhardt and myself – in the very same role – the supreme test – within a few days?

Now what could you write? – pray tell? – what could you possibly know how to write? What could you do but cheapen an already cheapened affair? A little boy stirring a stick in a puddle of mud.

*The peacock jumped off a cliff
and fell to the ground.*

Sometimes he looks into my eyes. What does he see? – what does he see? I tell him there is no me – at least there was none until I met him – until I met him, I always felt that there was no me. Is he seeing Cleopatra? – he never tells me what he sees. Is he seeing Electra? – Medea? Why the need to look so deeply? He never tells me what he is seeking, but I assume that he is searching for the roles he is writing for me. He holds the candle at arm's length – he moves it back and forth – from his right hand to his left and back again. When he has seen what he needs to see, he snuffs the flame.

The most beautiful promises offered by art.

My husband – Checchi. I barely give him a thought. He gave me Enrichetta. He gave me stability when I needed it and was in the way when I needed something else. The occasional letter from him, about Enrichetta, from South America. I encourage her to write to her father. I occasionally write a brief note, myself. Some day, I must look up the definition of 'divorce'. The mist fades from the mind as the sun comes up.

The husband's loyal servant proved to be disloyal. He poured his poison into the husband's ear. Circumstances seemed to make the young lady look guilty. All she had as proof of her loyalty was her word.

Nurturing, encouraging, supporting.
Making art is making love.

"Sarah Bernhardt is always Sarah Bernhardt. The dress, the title of the play, the order of the words may vary, but the woman is always the same. She does not enter into the leading character: she substitutes herself for it. All of this does not happen in the case of Duse, whose every part is a separate creation. Every idea, every shade of thought and mood, expresses itself delicately to the eye. Madame Bernhardt is a child beside her. Duse is ambidextrous and supple, like a gymnast or a panther, as the multitude of ideas finds physical expression in her movements. The indescribable distinction of Duse's acting is that every stroke of it is a distinctive human idea. Duse, with a tremor of the lip, which you feel rather than see, and which lasts half an instant, touches you straight on the very heart."

Ours for a life-time - i think and i feel - claims to know the future - how you mock me - i inhabit other worlds - poisoned by art - studying my face - signs another's name - hear a little bit more - the performance of your life.

Your friend has poured water into the wine. A gallon of water into a glass. You would water it down again with your little pen.

Don't you see? – don't you see? The self is all I have – this 'me' is all I own. This 'I' is the only thing I have in my hands.

He tried to snatch the gem away, but he failed to do so. Now he pours a gallon of ink over my memories. If I read it – this novel would blur my sense of my soul.

The peasant walked on the robe
that kept him dry.

The young poet was alone among the statues. At that moment he heard music from the Hall of the Greater Council. Violins, viols, violonchelos sang in turn. Trumpet blasts, a whole quartette, a thrilling chord. The lyric moment was like a religious ecstasy. He savoured the speech in which he had stirred the crowd with the images of an ideal life. He felt the immanent appearance of, as yet, an unknown muse.

The subterranean soul she must reveal.

Me, on stage, in London, at the Drury Lane theatre. Across the street from the theatre where Sarah plays. Marguerite in *La Dame di Camellias*. A French lady speaking in Italian. Marguerite and I as Marguerite on the stage. Marguerite takes over my body – Marguerite takes over my mind. I fall in love, each night, anew, with Armand. I am not an actress on stage – I am a woman whose heart is breaking. There are nights when my lips so tremble, I can hardly speak. All I can manage to do is to whisper, 'Armand – Armand'. It is the battle of the divas – the battle of acting styles. The battle of the old and the new. Every night I am embattled – waves of ecstasy and waves of despair. Every night, I am another Marguerite.

Sleeping under fruit that hangs from trees.
A question of who owns the sun.
A person's life presented in a play.

Some are taken aback by what I give them to see. What is an actress who has no entrance? Sarah would have lit up the stage! Duse sat in a corner, at first, and said not a word! I start slowly and build and build. I let the story give me my cues. I take life from the play and pass it on to you. By the end of the play, I have them all in my palm.

This is often the way things happen.
The mask will choose the face.
Think of yourself as having been chosen.
The mask has taken a liking to you.

Is not the poet a vindictive person?
Was revenge on Sarah not his original plan?

Until he turned his poison pen to revenge on you?

Romeo looks up and speaks his lines and I am enchanted. It is the moment to which all my fourteen years have moved. I reach in my basket and clasp a handful of rose-petals. I lean over and let a few of the rose-petals fall. He climbs up the vine-stalk to my room.

Over here was the altercation.
Tybalt was stabbed and lost his life.
If you look you can still see blood on some of the stones.

She never saw herself as a celebrity. Publicity was a chore that she would shun. No one knew what she did when she was not acting. She was never known to give an interview. She said 'when off the stage, I do not exist'.

A look – and I sought your eyes. A word – and I sought your lips. A tear – and I sought your sorrow. A smile – and I sought your joy. I was vulnerable the day I met your ghost.

The funeral train of the dead summer.
A funeral barge robed in golden draperies.
A Lorendana, a Morosina or a Soranza.

Oh I don't envy anyone in the world today. The sun is shining – the sky is blue – the birds are singing. We dwell in adjacent villas – in the hills, far above Florence, with a beautiful view. He has quiet for his writing. We meet any time that we please. I chill the wine, I order the flowers, I write the cheques. I am his help-meet in everything he needs. To serve one's country, to serve one's art, to serve one's love. Oh tell me, what could possibly be better than this? No – I don't envy anyone in the world.
All the truth contained in a stone.
A series of leavings-behind. Links in a chain as relentless as steel. Me – the child in a cold hotel-room. My mother – my father – left in turn. My lovers all leave me and I leave them. Enrichetta – now – in a convent. I can afford for her the best. Kindness, please – kindness, please. She is my own little girl. I cannot take her on the road. I must leave her here at the mercy of your care.

The lady tried to live her life through the lives of others. She manipulated their lives as much as she could. She encouraged a young writer of infinite promise. She discouraged a mousy woman whose life was drab.

"The applause for La Duse was enough to make the theatre shake."
"She was called out on stage – depleted – as limp as a rag."

I never see Marguerite Gautier – I wonder where she has gone. She used to be quite a fixture. Young Armand still frequents the tables. I must catch myself up with the gossip. These great loves are here for the moment – and then they are gone.

Even you, even you - half of myself - what was the plan - refuse to flow - the same old words - the chemicals of the brain - what door, i wonder - ask you some pertinent questions - your own true cause - a vision of the summer.

I must preserve my sense of self. I must go out again on the stage. I must be Phedre – Hedda – Medea – I must be me.

But do you see what I am saying? It's simply this. I think that I should be the one to decide how I am to be perceived.

Perceived by others. Perceived by the world. Perceived by writers – such as this shallow poet you seem so intent on giving a voice.

Every morning
the ink on the paper
would be gone.

The young poet approached the threshold – he moved through the throng. He penetrated the hall and stood by the platform with the orchestra and the singers. He searched for the tragic actress, but he could not find her. Where was she? – to what place had she withdrawn? – had she, perhaps, stepped outside for a little air? He felt confused – he felt anxious – where had she gone? The tragic actress was failing him when he needed her most.

Arranged with the symmetry of a fine keel.

A review from George Bernard Shaw. He has watched Sarah – he has watched me. I read the papers over an English cup of tea. 'Sarah does not enter into the leading character; she substitutes herself for it.' 'Duse, with a tremor of her lip, makes you feel rather than see.' 'Madame Bernhardt's clever performance was annihilated by Duse.' 'Duse provided the best modern acting I have seen.' 'Duse touches you straight to the heart.' I smile as I sip my English tea. This is the review that I shall save. I shall treasure the words of George Bernard Shaw.

The man from the bank loaned the young wife and mother the money. She signed a document on which she forged her father's name. The young wife didn't know that this was illegal. Now the man had her firmly in his grasp.

Seeking the plays that appeal to my essence.
Pouring my essence into those plays.

There is broken glass on the stage at times! I walk gingerly around the fragments of the life I live every day, as I try to remember and speak the words of the evening's play! I try so hard to be the character! – I try so hard not to be myself! Oh how I wish that I could participate in this play! But the fragments of my own life litter the stage!

Some other me - would call a coincidence - a fresh breeze - an invalid left behind - dipped in acid - will now be closed - kiss me awake - an unanswerable question - flew in the same sky - think of yourself.

And ultimately – this is the crux – this is the topic – this is the matter. Ultimately I am the one to decide how I am to be perceived – by me.

I own myself – do you see? I own myself when I am at home. I own myself when I am out in the world.

Would I not defend myself – when out in public – from a thief who attempts to snatch my purse? Would I not bar the door against a marauder who seeks to invade my home? Would I not resist the hand that reaches into my chest and feels around for the heart that it would seize?

She owned the sun; he owned the moon.
In her absence, he was dark.

My love reads to me sometimes. Passages from the developing novel. Some of the elder and some of the younger muse. He dips his pen in poison for the one who is based on the women of his past. He dips his pen in ambrosia for the one who is based on me. Oh, I am aware of the bobbing females in his wake. But he and I are like gods – our love is immortal – our pact is of iron. Every one of them has failed him – I am the only one who has not. We are partners in our bed and in our art.

But a contrary thought whispered.

A manager lights up a cigar. He says he will book me into every large city in the United States. He says there is a large Italian community in every one. He says he wants me to do many interviews. He says he wants me to do *La Dame aux Camellias* in every town. He says he will make me popular in America. He says he knows how a dollar is made.

The dog's

Shaking off a yoke of burdens.
A house that tumbles into the cellar.
A lady with a story she is reluctant to tell.

mouth

What reward for the young reporter if he chooses to help you?

What reward for him if he chooses to help someone else?
What is in it for him if he chooses to help himself?

watered.

The hall was completely silent – like the silence before his speech. Someone whispered a name and all eyes turned and looked. The youthful singer was hidden amid a quivering forest of bows. Then she appeared and began to sing – a transfiguring, timeless song. Sun on the mountains – sun on the sails – the words of the gods enchanting the ear. The secret music that dwelt within her touched his soul.

I will not drink of that fountain.

The theatre-world is mine. I have battled Sarah on her own turf and won the draw. Sarah is the old as I am the new. I can play Shakespeare – I can play Ibsen – I can play Racine. And I can play Marguerite as a human being. No need to strut and gesture and pose. Simply breathe out and simply breathe in. Underneath the layers of lacquer which are applied each time she is played, there is a lady who actually lived that life in her time. All one has to do is go back and bring her to life.

Chapter 9

He has buried himself in books. The best that can be found. All of the treasures of Antiquity that the libraries and the bookstores can yield. He is soaking himself in the great authors and their works. He has all of the imagery of the ages at his fingertips. He has watched me in the theatre – lingering silently in the wings – drunk in the ambiance of the ways of the stage. His plays will be towers in the desert. He is my own personal Shakespeare! – my own personal Aeschylus! – my own Racine!

I want you to tell me everything.

Plans to travel all over the world. London – Paris – Vienna – St. Petersburg. South America – Russia – the United States. Are audiences all the same or are they different, I am asked. How am I to know? – I do not sit in the audience – I am on stage. I am a person alive on stage – there is no audience for me – no, none at all.

Two tiny points of light

A crowd gathered in Venice beside the canal.
A question of poison or champagne.
A young man flinging a hand-ful of coins.

to serve

You have a rivalry with another actress?
You have both been called the best actress of these times?
Is that a fair assertion for me to make?

as beacons.

A coffin of opaline crystal.
Submerged in the waters of the lagoon.
Looking through transparent eyelids.

Oh my love is so extravagant. He wants nothing but the best for me. He wants his villa to be perfect when I visit him – after his creative work for the day is done. Furniture, carpets, vases – paintings, curtains, antique clocks. He pictures me against these backdrops in the roles he is writing for me. Sometimes when we make love, he stops and jots a new idea. I tell him I am not jealous – I tell him I trust my love completely – his other ladies are the roles that I shall play. He is a genius and I am his serving-maid.

Everything I think of seems so silly and insignificant.

I like to play Nora as young. I feel young when I play her. I always enjoy the taste of macaroons. Ibsen has quite a sense of humour. Some have said that I make the early scenes too light. But Nora – little Nora and I – are in our own little world. We know each other's thoughts at every stage.

The young girl returned the prince's letters. She told him that she had once believed his words. He told her that once he had loved her. He told her that he had loved her not.

"Duse is elegant without affectation, and beautiful without cosmetics."

"It is all in her voice and her deep, black eyes."

A hand is beckoning me! It is the hand of my companion, although I cannot see his face! He moves towards a shrubbery of box and hornbeams! It appears to be an overgrown, abandoned labyrinth from former days! There is a rusty iron gate! My companion pushes open the gate and waves me inside!

Life reveals itself - sunk beneath the waves - give me my cues - to find the words - using my power - show the humanity - whose keeper i have been - vendors of scurrility - sense of beauty of thought - the blinding light.

This poet that you rate so highly. He wanted to write his own great roles. He knew that I had acted all the greatest roles on the stage.

But he had no such greatness in him. He thought that I could supply his want. He thought that I – the essence of me – could activate him.

But the flaw, you see. Yes, and it was fatal. Was in his conception of life as a role.

The great characters are not simply roles. Though that is the story of Bernhardt's career. The great characters are actually ourselves on the stage.

We don't act these roles – we live them. They become us and we become them. If all they are is a costume and makeup – Sarah Bernhardt's conception again – then they are nothing but a mask that a child would wear.

It is an exchange at the deepest level. Blood for blood and bone for bone. Marrow for marrow – yes – and the chemicals of the brain.

Hedda Gabler lives in me and I in her. She knows that Sarah has nothing to offer. A little sister wearing her big sister's clothes.

Hedda waits, each night, for me – in the dark. She waits for the lights to come up on stage. She knows that we only live when we are together.

There is only one Hedda Gabler – there is only one Eleonora Duse. I am half of myself in the dressing room – a costume and nothing else. Hedda is half of herself in the dark while waiting on stage.

Our soul – our single-soul – is only alive for an hour or two. We speak the lines that are our life-blood. We are together – as one – again. We die as we take our bows at the end of the play.

When the eagle looked for its wings
they were gone.

He keeps a strict regimen – time for writing; time for me. He says that it is the thought of me that inspires. He cannot write when anyone else is in his presence. I respect what he has to say. I busy myself with other things. He gives no inkling of what he is writing. He says he carries it all inside. A boiling cauldron of gold in the alchemist's mind. I shall not set eyes on the plays, he says, until every golden word is in its place.

I was green in judgement, cold in blood, to say as I said then.

Asking Boito for a token to add to my collection. Something precious to him, though completely unknown to me. The more mysterious the better – it will fill some empty hours. I shall place it on my table as I place my other gems. 'Something that speaks' is all I wrote in the note that I sent. His note to me was addressed to me in my married name.

Why did she promote a disgraced man's cause? Where was the magic handkerchief? The young woman chided her husband. Why turn your mind against your own true cause?

Placing myself in the hands of another.
Feeling the need of no other hands.

I am standing at the old rusty gate of an abandoned labyrinth! Instinctively, I shrink back in fear! My companion moves deeper inside and waves for me to follow! 'Come in and look for me!' laughs the voice of my companion! 'Look for me and I shall look for Ariadne!' My mind is filled with misery! – terror! – fear!

What, then, would be left - the centre of all the lines - she could trans-
form herself - alive and breathing - a restless woman - nurse that dream - gives
no inkling - sunshine and rose-petals - his salacious drivel - my birthplace, my

balcony, my tomb.

You seem like a very intelligent fellow. You have impressed me. Not so much by your words – I barely listen as you speak – but by the way you simply sit and wait and take it all in.

You are like that mirror over there – the big one on the wall, near the clock. That mirror says nothing – even when I ask it for advice. It simply sits and waits – watches and takes it all in. It gathers information and then it thinks.

Or – perhaps it doesn't think! Perhaps you don't think! Perhaps no one thinks!

Perhaps everyone gathers information! Baskets of information! – from the land, from the air, from the sea! And the information simply sits in the baskets – unused!

The handsome peasant
bowed to the Queen.

Swords and pistols and shields and bucklers, whenever I visit his sumptuous abode. He says he writes much better if he is surrounded by these things. They are the ambiance that gives him what he needs. He writes from sun-up 'til our tryst-time – after I leave he writes again. He writes all night, he tells me, and then makes love to me. I feel as if I am on Olympus – a stealthy visit to one of the gods. Only once in a generation – only once in a hundred years – does nature produce such a Titan as is he. Every thought while he is writing – he assures me again and again – is focussed on the great roles he is writing for me.

I please where I am most bound to please.

Oh how I enjoy the simple situation. I am a child and I am expected to act as a child. It is a very seductive experience. Torvald loves me in this mode. He loves to play inside the doll's house. He loves to admonish and instruct. He would never suspect that he is a doll as well. I take his orders with a grain of salt, of course, but I like to be told what to do. The chick sings the happiest tunes inside the shell.

A guard who blocks a back-stage door.
Adjusting one's choice of parts.
Clutching the truth with talons.

Oh the lies that I would be accused of telling, were I ever to speak in my own true voice. That is why I never tell my thoughts out loud. Suppose I were interviewed and I said that I have never sought success? That the theatre for me is a refuge and that is all? What kind of thought is that to speak in an interview? My thoughts are in a cave – I have rolled a huge rock across. The price of a ticket has limited access. There is no entrance to the world behind the stage.

All shall be well, the mask-master chuckles.
It seems the mask has chosen you.
In time you shall be free, of course.
But first, I must ask you to pay.

The actress to whom I am referring is, of course, Sarah Bernhardt? You often act in the same towns and in the same plays? Is this planned – or what you would call a coincidence?

So – what led me to buy the roses? Well – my father was standing in a courtyard. And it was a beautiful sunny day. And down from above came a shower of rose-petals. The petals landed on his shoulders and at his feet.

This is the house where Juliet lived.
Have your tickets in your hands.
It looked much the same on the night of the Capulet ball.

There was another famous actress. She, too, was born for the stage. Her reputation kept growing and growing. Each would read the other's reviews. Their eyes would flash in fury as they read the words.

There are rivers in the jungle. Ways in and ways out. I hack and chop my way through the underbrush. Blistering sun – pouring rain. I have never found a river. I am looking still.

The supple movement of the seaweed.
The undulating tresses of her hair.
The sun of the resurrected dawn.

It was the days of the merchant princes. A ship arrived from the farthest seas. A young girl clutched a token in her hand. The sight of the city took her breath away. She pressed herself against the rail. The precious token slipped from her hand. It caught the sunlight as it slipped into the lagoon. She lived in Venice for the rest of her life. Every night she saw the token in her dreams.

My lover asks for a solemn promise. Our pact must be as iron. We are the two whose names will live 'til the end of time. That he will always write plays for me – that I will always act in his plays – that I am trusting him to write my greatest roles. Whatever is new is bound to be difficult – he has gathered-in baskets of pearls. The best of Shakespeare – the best of Euripides

– the best of Racine. When has greatness not had a struggle to break the shell?

These deeds must not be thought after these ways.

My visits with my daughter, Enrichetta, are always less than satisfactory. I see her as often and as little as I can. I don't know what I want from her – I don't know what she wants from me. I want her to live the childhood that I never had – far away from the rag-tag vagabonds of the travelling circus-act. I never, ever want her to trod the boards. She will be an actual person – not at all like me.

Have I not seen the fall of Ilium?

Woman is cursed by man and by the gods. By the gods, who gave her man – by man for whom she thirsts. Nectar is poison and poison is nectar. Decent men are in short supply. Where will Enrichetta find a decent man?

The lady burned the young writer's precious manuscript. The lady threatened to burn the mousy lady's hair. She sneered at her husband's petty concerns. But nothing seemed to cure her sense of self.

"Duse does not shout, nor sob, nor sing."
"Her voice is as natural as if she is not an actress on stage."

My companion's laughter echoes through the labyrinth! I move deeper as I try to find the voice! I look for an opening in the hedge as I inch along! The laugher ceases! – all is still! The green walls hold me prisoner! – each corridor is narrower and narrower still! No companion! – no Ariadne! – I despair of ever finding the rusty iron gate!

Other half of my soul - takes life from that heart - never remove the shutters - wave after wave - we live inside - a conspiracy of angels - splattered in ink - regained its spirit - plenty left to say - all is contingent.

Oh I don't think I'm making myself very clear. I don't think I'm getting through to you at all. A total failure to communicate on my part.

For you to get to know me would be nothing. You must get to know yourself. That is what your paper-thin poet did not understand.

Oh he was shallow – miserably shallow. He sought to borrow a human essence – as one would borrow a cup of sugar at one's door. He had no key to unlock the cupboard of the self.

Every morning
the ink in the inkwell
would glow.

Almost complete, my lover tells me. He will have something to show me soon. For the present, he feels the need to get away. He needs to read and think and polish. Make the work as perfect as can be. Trust me, trust me, trust me, trust me, he whispers over and over again. The work of these days will catapult us up among the stars. A little time apart, while I refine our enterprise. One last kiss as he mounts his horse. He reminds me of how I like to be surprised.

What means this, my lord?

The house is tumbling around me. The ceiling-timbers crash to the floor. The floorboards open up and I tumble through. The doll's house that Torvald built has been shaken by a subtle breeze. A simple puff of wind on a quiet day. Take a broom and sweep the debris from the cellar floor. Oh who to blame – Torvald or I? Or my father? – or society? – or no one at all? It was Torvald who built the doll's house, but it was I who passed the hammer and the nails.

The young wife and mother tried to pay the huge debt but was never able. She had never been taught the financial side of life. She was all alone in the world with her dilemma. All she knew was that her husband must never know.

Performing on all the stages of the world.
Living my life solely on the stage.

Oh you must let me paint your face.
All the children have been painted.
I have all the colours I need right here in this box.
It will be my version of you.
Though it will still be you, I assure you, underneath.

The essence – the core – the root - mind was being poisoned - what is it called - all of my true thoughts - to come out alive - speaking different words - a briar of tangled thorns - regain his lost love - every town in the world - standing on that precipice.

Oh I should write a shallow book. Not about me – but about your 'great poet'. It would be shallow and sentimental and foolish and trite. Observations – gestures and tics. Tricks of voice – habitual sayings – a way of holding a glass of wine. All the things that Sarah Bernhardt knows how to do.

All the outside – all the surface. The costume hanging on a hook. Exactly the hollow, shallow treatment he has given to me.

I'll call it 'art'– I'll call it 'great art'. I shall give interviews galore. I'll say it's the essence of the man I used to know.

And people like you – the popular press – will take me at my word. A little canary in a cage – with a sign that says 'The Eagle – The Greatest of Birds'. People will line up and pay a penny to have a look.

She owned the sun; he owned the moon.
One day he stole her keys.

Oh where is my lover? – I do not know. Oh where is my lover? – I cannot say. Gone from my sight – gone from my presence – but not from my thoughts. I hug the pillows that he has hugged – I sip the wine of our sacred toasts – I sit and wait by the window for him to come home. Wherever he is – wherever he travels – whatever duty he now performs, I know that every thought in his mind is of me.

What sort of days do you imagine I spend?

Playing all the greatest roles in all the premier theatres. I have become – at last – the actress I was born to be. Bringing myself alive on stage – bringing the audiences alive as what they have never considered themselves to be. They must see themselves as Hedda, Nora, Cleopatra – see themselves as Ophelia, Medea, Electra – see themselves as the person who is me. All of life has happened to these characters in these dramas. All of life is happening to the people out there in the seats. The theatre is not for entertainment – not for superficial concerns. Life is agony – life is ecstasy. Never forget that you are on stage and the world is on fire.

It savoured

A hand pouring water into wine.
A person lazing on a bridge.
Bonfires being lit with shouts of joy.

the saliva

Do you, yourself, see your relationship as a rivalry?
Or do you see it as a stimulus for both of you to excel?
Is there anything on the topic that you would care to say?

between its fangs.

Betrayed! – betrayed! – betrayed! He skedaddled off to Paris when I turned my back! He has offered Sarah my part in our new play! She is staging it in her theatre! It will be a gaudy display! – a three-ring circus with elephants, clowns and acrobats! My greatest love is my greatest betrayer! – he prefers Sarah's acting to mine! An inch of make-up and the hands that saw the air! I wait for the telegrammed report on opening night. A group of 'friends' has come to comfort me – to watch me perform as I choke on the news. I sit uncomfortably in the chair with a knife in my back.

Now we've killed two birds with one stone.

A break is not a break unless it is final and clean and pure. Whatever blood falls on the carpet is lost and gone. Bandages cover but they do not heal. Healing is what takes place inside. I practice slamming the door when I am alone. As soon as Torvald comes in, I shall start my diatribe. I shall be right and he shall be wrong – he shall be weak and I shall be strong. I shall take this axe and sever my own right arm.

Chapter 10

He comes whining back to apologize. A dog with his tail between his legs. Oh I admit that I have betrayed you! Hate me! hate me! hate me! I deserve no less than that! I thought that Sarah would put it over, but she failed miserably in the part! Everyone says that she is a great actress! – but she is shallow compared to you! I realized that as soon as she stepped on the stage! She has none of your depth or gravity! – you alone can play this part! The play is ours! – the part is yours! – I am wearing a hair shirt! You inspired me! – I turned my back on you! – I would see the justice if you were to do the same!

Burning together in eternal truth.

Touring South America. Montevideo – Rio Di Janeiro – Buenos Aires – Sao Paulo. *Fedora – Denise – Fernande* – every play is welcome, it seems. Huge theatres – huge audiences – huge box-office – small earnings. A determination to form my own company with my own ledger. Gaining a continent and shedding a husband. Fending off gossip from the newspapers on my return.

Beacons to guide

A young actress paying her dues in small roles.
A husband who provides a safe home.
Smears of pain daubed on walls.

each word and gesture

What does it matter to you what others think of you?
What do the tabloid newspaper writers think of you?
What do the audiences think of you when you are on stage?

in every play.

The vision of the beautiful dead.
A file of boats dressed with fruit.
The chronicles of the Doges.

The young poet descended to the Venetian courtyard. He hid in a shadowy corner and watched the crowd. He was about to meet the two women – the older and the younger. The chorus of the populace had echoed through the harbour of San Marco. His speech had kissed the essence of Venice awake. Why had the actress arranged for him to meet the girl?

The rich jewels that illuminate the night.

Battling with the playwrights! Do not water down the classics to make them palatable on the stage! Do not strip them bare as you turn them into Italian for me to act! Give them to me as they were written! Give me Shakespeare! – give me Racine! It is I who shall make them palatable to an audience! Not by giving them water! – by giving them wine!

The young girl was disturbed. Things were turning out quite wrong. Why had the dream become a nightmare? Who would have thought that this would be?

"Duse lives every part and that is dangerous for an actress."

"Some nights she is marvelous and some nights she should have stayed home."

"I doubt whether any of us realized, after seeing Madame Bernhardt's very clever performance as Magda on Monday night, that there was room in the nature of things for its annihilation within forty-eight hours by so comparatively quiet a talent as Duse's. And yet annihilation is the only word for it. Sarah was very charming, very jolly when the sun shone, very petulant when the clouds covered it, and positively angry when they wanted to take her child from her, but she did not trouble us with any fuss about the main theme of the play."

News of my actions - the woman is always the same - approached the threshold - has all the imagery - thought long and hard - through my eyelids - forming in his mind - waves of ecstasy - a quiet bay - the mask has chosen you.

Do you see what has happened? – I have not been a person to the public at all. The public craves personal trivia – it is Sarah's stock-in-trade. And the little scribbler has offered to fill the void.

But who, then, am I if not the creature in the novel? Who is it that lives and breathes inside this skin? Who is the creature that he utterly – willfully – tragically – failed to perceive?

I am nothing as I sit here, in the public mind. Do you understand what I mean? I do not exist when I am not on stage.

Two creatures hobbling helplessly,
unable – alas – to fly.

My lover shares his thoughts with me. I am getting my revenge on Sarah. I am making her the villain of my new novel. The failed muse – the aging actress – whose magic fizzled when I called on her for help. You, my dear, are still the younger muse. The actress in the bloom of her prime. You are doing for me what Sarah couldn't do. I am tracing her every wrinkle with the nib of my pen.

All is abolished – all is vanished.

Boito, Boito, Boito. Have I seduced him or has he seduced me? He is older, sophisticated – a man of influence. I am young, artistic – I have my charms. A very useful intertwining I am sure. I have seen it in the theatre many times. Seeking the sun together – until one vine climbs higher on the tree.

The young lady was disturbed. Things were turning out quite wrong. Why had the dream become a nightmare? Who would have thought that this would be?

Broken branches in the orchard after a windstorm.
Nurturing them – together – back to life.

As my sister's life was poisoned, so shall this tip be poisoned too. She spent her life in service – as have I – as have I. By this act shall the poison from my life be drained. Never shall master serve the servant – the master would rather die than serve. By this poison shall the servant set himself free.

Someone different every night - an overgrown, abandoned labyrinth - it is a knife - how am i to know - an entirely new kind of acting - the anguish and the anxiety - flutter down from a balcony - in a cocoon - to live a good life - considered myself to be free.

Whatever he has written is a fiction. Words from air – ink from an empty bottle. A character whom he has created for an imaginary stage.

There are those of us who do not express ourselves in the language of the everyday. How I sit and sip my tea – how I talk to a young reporter. No – we express ourselves in the language of the great lives that we lead on stage.

I am not me when I eat my grapefruit. That me is the dressing gown which I leave on a hook on the dressing-room door. That is the me that you are interviewing now.

Then he mounted the Queen's horse
and rode away.

The young poet was ecstatic in the glow of the torches. The cries of the crowd were still ringing in his ears. In his mind persisted an image of the young singer. She had drawn on hidden music within herself. She had filled him with a superabundance of life. Here she was at the top of the staircase – enveloped in white.

The fruits of the earth and the sea.

The joys and chores of having my own acting troupe. Hiring the right people – that, I find, is the key. Not always easy – not always possible, it seems. Attempting to undo – in rehearsal – years of stumbling, blundering behavior on the stage. The striking of poses – the facial contortions – the little tricks that coax the audience to spontaneous applause. All of these I must strip right down to the bone.

A light left burning in a room.
A statue which heaves the occasional sigh.
Something that does not depend on thinking.

My life is all bits and pieces. My life has no spinal thread – whether red or silver or gold or black or brown. I live in hotel rooms – I live in villas – I live in an apartment on the canal. I have less than the poorest drudge of a gondolier. My daughter writes me letters – where would I put her if she should come? What would I say to her if I brought her to live with me? I fling my script across the room – tempted to throw it into the fire. I pick it up and I slump in my chair – it is the only thing I can cling to in my despair.

My mind is in a panic.
I don't know what to do.
Why should I pay for a mask I don't fancy?
How could a mask have chosen me?

What did your lovers think of you?
What did the poet think of you then – think of you now?
What do you think this young reporter thinks of you?

It was my mother – on a balcony – looking down. She was Angelica Cappelletto – that was her name. The same name as Juliet. They met and they were married – and not long after that union, I – Juliet-Duse – was born.

It is springtime in Verona.
Here there is love and there is hate.
Verona seems to be every town in the world.

A great rivalry sprang up between the two. They presented their plays in the same cities. They played the same great roles. There was a great demand for tickets. Every theatre seat was filled.

Tears run down my cheeks like boulders down a mountain. Each one smashes to pieces on the rocks below. I have been standing here for a long time now. I have nowhere else to go. I am up to my waist in broken tears.

The price of the golden robe.
A percentage of the tax on fruit.
Pomona paying tribute to Ariadne.

His apology has made us stronger. Best that he did just exactly what he did. People must tire of my denigration of Sarah. Now he knows her for what she is. He appreciates me more after seeing her fail in our play. She is for tearing the scenery to tatters – knows all the tricks of the conjurer's trade. A mere performer – as I am an actress. He is a boy – a clumsy boy – with a grown-up's desires. He fell off the cloud and I grabbed him by the scruff of his shirt. No doubt our bond is stronger than it ever was before.

The illusion of the moment was abolished.

Going to see my Enrichetta. She always says that she is happy at school. It is raining, so we hold our meeting inside. A large empty room – a stage at one end. The rain-drops run down the window-pane. She tells me that she is happy at her school.

The lady was disturbed. Things were turning out quite wrong. Why had the dream become a nightmare? Who would have thought that this would be?

"Duse plays Sardou and Dumas with Ibsen's psychology."
"In an Ibsen play, she is the essence of Ibsen himself."

"Duse, on the other hand, with one look at the father, nailed the theme of the play to the stage as the subject of the impending dramatic struggle, before she had been five minutes on the scene. Before long, there came a stroke of acting which will probably never be forgotten by those who saw it, and which explained at once why those artifices of the dressing-table which help Madame Bernhardt would hinder Duse almost as much as a screen being placed in front of her."

I am not she - tear open your chest - who would have thought - make it walk and make it talk - at its height that day - had a terrible shock - serve your greater ends - melt into my skin - approved by me - uncertain of the other.

Don't make the mistake that he has made – if what you say about the novel is true. Don't write of a dressing gown – draped over an empty chair – while the real me is expressed in Phedre, Iphigenia, Lady Macbeth, alive on the stage.

Don't you hear – as you sit and listen in this room – this empty dressing room – the great applause and the endless cheers? Don't you want a seat on the balcony? Don't you want to see the real me – the essence – the core – the root – as I live – really, truly live – on the stage?

I have been animated by Racine – by Corneille. By Shakespeare himself. How could I have been brought to life by a petty scribbler? – who couldn't tell a bauble from a gem?

It was a game
that the faeries
liked to play.

The aging actress had been smiling at him as he spoke to the assemblage. In his mind crowded images of distress. Poisoned by art – wrinkled by age – worldly corruption on eloquent lips. The gift of a heart that was no longer young. Dry hands that were pressing juice from deceitful fruits. Here she was at the top of the staircase – smiling at him.

The trees felt their leaves dying on the branches.

I speak Italian in English plays – I speak in Italian in French plays. Phedre, Cleopatra, Electra – Medea, Magda, Marguerite. I am only a pale imitation. All of my characters think in English and French and Greek. There have been many great Italians. Women of heart and women of soul. Where are the playwrights who can put these souls on the stage?

The young wife and mother was disturbed. Things were turning out quite wrong. Why had the dream become a nightmare? Who would have thought that this would be?

Re-imagining the roles of the greatest playwrights.
Stripping the surface back and boring down to the core.

The bell sounded at midnight. They had gone for a gondola ride. The beauty of the waters – the echoing sound in the canal. They felt the reverberation in the roots of their hair. Their spirits rushed together. They gazed deeply into each other's eyes. They leaned towards each other and embraced. Drinking deep, they were still athirst. Their breaths mingled as they sighed. Ours for an hour – ours for a life-time. Our embrace will make us divine. Each one kept repeating – let me serve! – let me serve! Perfect love – perfect love – perfect life.

Shaken by a subtle breeze - a very shallow play - your elbow knocks one over - nothing as i sit here - the secret music - steel yourself with armour - ship that keeps its course - perhaps no one thinks - strip right down to the bone - gone from my sight.

No! – I have never read the novel! I have no interest at all! How could I read a shallow fiction when I have lived all the great roles?

He couldn't climb with me to the heavens. He couldn't descend with me to the pit. So what do you think are the chances, then, for you?

No – you don't want to interview me. It is a briar of tangled thorns – a crevice in a field of ice. A valley deeper than the one they call 'death' in the United States.

He took the sun; he kept the moon.
Now she sits in the dark.

Soon I'll be acting in our plays. Finally ready to put them on the stage. Reading the scripts. Hiring the actors. Having the sets built. No expense will be too great – not a penny shall be spared. It will be a triple coronation – a crown for me, a crown for D'Annunzio, a crown for Italy. I shall take these plays to the ends of the theatrical earth. Not a theatre that shall not resound with applause. D'Annunzio! – D'Annunzio! – D'Annunzio! My lover's name shall be the wine on everyone's lips.

I will reflect forever thy luminous image.

I seldom read the reviews. When I do, I am pleased enough. A handful of reviewers appreciate what I am trying to do. A few seem pleased when they catch me on an off-night – when the sap refuses to flow – and a few sigh openly for the likes of Sarah's histrionics. But really, I am served well enough in that regard. Shallow-good or shallow-bad is nothing to me. I am the new, alternative fad to Sarah's fading fad. In any case, I seldom read the reviews.

The dog

A young wife who signs another's name.
Wondering whether the gods have actually spoken.
A boulder rolling down a cliff.

was about to bolt

What did your parents think of you?
What did your husband think of you then – think of you now?
What does your daughter, in the convent, think of you?

the piece of meat.

The two women stood at the top of the staircase. The young singer and the aging actress. He sensed a secret soul in the furthermost depths of his being. A work of art that he knew he could not accomplish alone. Oh why was the actress so insistent on this meeting? – placing herself in such a position? – her worldly wisdom and despair beside the splendour of innocent youth? She introduced him as 'the master of the flame'.

The myth of the pomegranate was revivified.

I have heard of this fellow, D'Annunzio. A writer, so they say, of impassioned and stirring verse. Italy needs a classical repertoire. I am so tired of insipid plays. I wonder if he could write for the theatre? Perhaps if someone who knew the theatre could act as his muse.

Chapter 11

Setting off on a great adventure. The dawn of a whole new era – a new constellation in the sky. A series of great Italian plays – with Italian settings and Italian stories – Italian characters who speak Italian words. Every word was written by that great new classical dramatist – Gabrielle D'Annunzio. He will take his place with Ibsen and Shakespeare in the sky. Embodied, on the stage, for all to see, in human form, by La Duse – an Italian – an Italian through and through.

To be able to be free from care, quite free from care.

Touring Egypt and touring Russia. Taking the plays to the ends of the earth. I am the owner of my own acting troupe. I decide on the plays, I hire the actors, I rehearse them in their parts. Pleased to think that I can make changes in the company and the repertoire. Pleased to think that whatever happens – whatever triumphs or whatever defeats – will be mine and mine alone from this day on. Every prop, every costume, every set is approved by me. Mixing art and entertainment. *Divorcons – Antony and Cleopatra – Tristi Amori – A Doll's House – Frou-frou –* and on and on and on. Poised on a knife edge – walking a tightrope – juggling entertainment and art. Keeping in mind that many acting troupes have failed.

You never know

Plays that fail on the stage.
Lovers who speak their thoughts in rhyme.
Cracks in a marble statue.

if you are going

May I ask about your relationship with your audiences?
You have played, so I gather, in all the major cities?
Do some people come to see you numerous times?

to come out alive.

The figure of the noble lady.
An allegory of Paolo Veronese.
Something fresh and rustic.

Presenting my lover's new play – our new play – *Sogno D'un Matteo Di Primavera* – in Paris. Here in the city alone, as my lover stays behind, in Italy, working on our next play. Not a play at all, but a dramatic monologue. Flowery, poetic – my lover's personality illuminates every word. My role is to provide a voice in which I have never spoken on stage. I struggle a bit, in rehearsal, to adjust my signature style. The audience is tepid – the reviews are a trifle unkind. 'Bizarre', 'morbid', 'infantile' – 'pretentious', 'abstract', 'turgid'. 'La Duse's power is largely wasted in this thin plot'. I can see Sarah smirking as I board the train. Oh I hope my lover never sees these reviews.

Now I feed myself with most delicious poison.

Getting ready for Cleopatra in my dressing room. Loose, flowing robes and a modest crown. I like to prowl around the stage. It makes the silence and the stillness more of a contrast. The male actors bluster and gesture and grimace and shout. One of the roles by which I seize and hold the stage.

The prince caught wind that the girl was acting as a spy. That she had chosen to be an agent of the king. He offended the girl with talk of country matters. He told her that all breeding is a sin.

"Duse plays what is individual."
"We in the audience experience what is universal."

I climb the highest mountain! I seek the wisest man! The climb is long and tiring! – I pause for bread and wine! The wise man sits on a dias! I bow and seek my boon! I ask him to eradicate my fears!

A transfiguring, timeless song - perceived by the world - her seeds of hope - slipped from her hand - desperate for joy - wearing a hair shirt - ultimately i am the one - make them your own - a fair comment - our single-soul.

Oh, I am trying as hard as I can to get to know you! I am trying to look at your mind through the holes in your eyes! Trying to look at all the creatures that swim in your skull!

Ever look through a microscope? Astonishing what you see. All these tiny creatures eking out a life.

Hold a lens up to your head. A very powerful lens. I promise you, you'll be surprised at what you see.

An ancient statue stood
in the courtyard.

My love looks at me closely. He seems to be studying my face. What age were you in 1883? Why, my love, do you ask? I have decided to set my new novel in that year. You recall, of course, that there will be two muses. The younger muse will be the age that you were that year.

God, yes! September already!

Boito, Boito, Boito. We meet in secret – we write our letters – the rest is silence. No one will ever know a thing about Boito and me.

What had her life been like in Venice? How did Venetian women act? The husband's mind was being poisoned. The husband was unable to keep control of his thoughts.

Acting in roles for which I feel completely unsuited.
Assuming that what is broken I can mend.

'Your fears, alas, can never be destroyed! But from your fears you can separate yourself! Put your fears in a bubble! Put the bubble in the river! The bubble will flow to the ocean! Your fears will evaporate and fall to the earth as rain!'

A weight lifting - drank the poison - take the blame himself - can see his soul - stirring the ashes - wandered across my stage - a distinctive human idea - no connection – whatsoever - the outskirts of verona - the sharpest of eyes.

The human being is amazing. We fool ourselves over and over again. We live inside, but we think we live outside.

We stumble through the forest. We plunge in fear down the waterfall. We swim for our lives when the lifeboat springs a leak.

But the greatest storms and sunsets. The greatest explosions and quietest songs. Are all right here behind these two eyes and between these two ears.

The ancient city stood
in spendour.

Presenting my lover's new play – our new play – *La Gioconda* – in Sicily. This time, an actual play. Closer to that which is expected to appear on the stage. My role is of a woman who becomes crippled while trying to save a work of art. There is a wall against which we are butting our heads. On the other side of that wall is the happy blend of entertainment and art. Each time I return home, my lover has a new play. All we need is one special play and we will break through. 'This unholy artistic pact between La Duse and this head-in-the-clouds playwright-manqué, D'Annunzio – in which she reportedly has taken a vow to act only in the works from his pen – will prove to be the cause of the demise of her once-great acting career.' The reviewers are crushing our project in the shell. I leave the reviews crumpled-up on the hotel-room floor.

But if you will allow me, I will speak truthfully.

Oh Antony! – Oh Antony! Don't you know that Cleopatra and I are Queen of Egypt – Queen of the Nile? Do you not know that Rome is not independent – cannot support herself? That she depends on others for sustenance – for wine and for bread? The Nile is ever-abundant, ever-fecund, ever-refreshed. You would do well to consider your relationship with the Nile.

> *An exhausted person flopping in a chair.*
> *A photograph of a mother and a daughter.*
> *A lady who is trying not to think.*

Unable to sleep at two a.m. Unable to sleep at three a.m. Unable to sleep at four a.m. Did I only dream that I had some sleep in between? The mind is a blank at such moments. Under torture I could not reveal what is wrong. All the cares of the world, perhaps – all those people whose lives have been cheated by faulty scales. Who – looking at me – would ever believe that I have any cause for concern?

> *I leave the shop in a hurry.*
> *I bang my shoulder against the door.*
> *The mask-master calls after me.*
> *Oh be assured you shall pay.*

Are you aware, when on stage, of individuals in the audience?
Are you aware that there is an audience at all?
Or do you forget that you are even in a play?

What happens to a person when they become another person? What stays and what leaves? What stays in each and what leaves from each? What did Juliet feel happening to her and what did I feel happening to me? I became Juliet and she became me.

> *Here is the kitchen where the feast was prepared.*
> *Marchpan and other fine foods.*
> *You can hear the laughter of Peter and the Nurse.*

Each felt she had bested in every encounter. Each saw herself as the diva of her time. Her rival was being praised for all the wrong reasons. It was a pity that this was the case. Who could sit in a theatre and not see what was on stage?

Destitute of all the things that matter. Surrounded – like a queen – by brilliance, in the fading candle-light. And not a drop or two of water or a crust of stale bread. Trapped in a store-room where they keep the crowns and the swords. The charming prince turned the lock and took the key.

The rich folds of heavy brocade.
The figs and grapes of Autumn.
A child with a picture-book.

My lover reads me some of his pages. The older muse has Sarah's features, my love, though I will never use her name. She will be old, tired, wrinkled – a spent force – a face-worn coin – an aging actress whose best days are now behind. I feel a slight twinge – but just a twinge – of sympathy for Sarah. How cruel, my love, you can be. Sarah is human – she is a woman – I'm sure she is very aware of her age. No doubt Sarah will be crushed when she hears what you've done – she'll rue the day when she ever set eyes on you.

It is a false steward that stole his master's daughter.

Father losing his sense of purpose. A kindly old man, bending close to the ground. He who used to be so tall, so handsome, so strong. Father whose keeper I have been since I was little more than a child. A rocking chair on a porch and a quiet farewell.

Ah, you have missed my meaning entirely.

My father did not want to be an actor. It was the profession of the family firm. Rattling wagon – moth-eaten costumes – tired mare. He did well for a wife and a young daughter on the most miserable of terms. There are no monuments to people like him. No days set aside on the national calendar. He did what he did and now he sleeps well in a comfortable grave.

There was a scandal that was not of the lady's doing. Word of the scandal was sure to spread throughout the town. The judge warned her that she was in danger of being ostracized. She would spend years perhaps, alone, in her husband's house.

"Duse plays the arid darkness behind the light laugh."
"Every night she is an actor in a passion play."

I bow and turn to leave, but the wise man speaks again! 'Next you must separate yourself! Put yourself in a bubble! Sit in the bubble – do not move! Do not think – do not breathe! Eat no bread and drink no wine for the rest of your life!'

Another fine mask - floorboards open up - better not to think - enjoyed all the perks - the simple situation - sole source of sustenance - a story that begins - is this a dagger - nothing but a mask - what do you call it.

I am an actress. I play many roles. Ever wonder what such a thing could mean?

I have been inside the minds of all the great women of the past. The women imagined by all the greatest artists. I have lived my life inside these women's skulls.

But – here's the catch, if you want to know. Here's the thing that is hard to grasp. All the writers of great female roles have been great men.

Dance and prance
upon the stage.

Presenting my lover's new play – our new play – *La Citta Morta* – in a number of Italian cities. My role is of a woman who shudders and shrieks and bellows the secrets of her soul. I make the effort to play this part. This woman is not me – I am not she, but this play is the presentation of my lover's mind and soul – in essence – on the stage. I will do everything I can to advance his career. 'This play – a fiasco for Sarah Bernhardt– is now a fiasco for La Duse.' 'The two greatest actresses of our time could not breathe life into this lifeless, dead, and unlamented play.' The financial returns are disappointing. I don't want my lover to be discouraged, so I assign him a larger portion out of my share.

From this time such I account thy love.

It is we who have taken you in – Cleopatra and I. You who were without a home – a waif in exile. We are the milk and the bread – we are the roof and the hearth. The cold rain beats on the walls and against the door.

The young wife's husband was honoured with a new position. His first act was to cut the staff at the bank. The man who was fired was the man who had loaned the young wife the money. This man now threatened the wife that he would send her to jail.

Complete control over my troupe and over my destiny.
Choosing plays, choosing roles, choosing life.

Being interviewed for the newspapers! The probing of a surgical knife! What part of me will you cut and take away? What of me will you place in the market on full display? Searching the streets of strange cities at midnight! – the rain in the gutters, the bone-chilling winds! – looking for the pieces of me that were taken away!

Dips his pen in poison - could not find the words - dwell in adjacent villas - an undeserving man - compares two performances - add to my collec-

tion - a chance to see - how i am to be perceived - a warm and friendly place - narrower and narrower still.

What good does it do me? This playing of roles? What do I know that no one else knows?

Do I know myself better than if I had never been on the stage? Do I know myself less than if I'd sold the tickets or swept the floor? What does an artist know that no one else can possibly know?

Someday I shall play the nurse – Juliet's nurse. When I get a few more laugh-lines on my brow. Sit in the sun and think my thoughts against the dove-cote wall.

Be the artist
on the highwire.

What to think at this stage of the game? Presenting my lover's new play – our new play – *Francesca da Rimini* – in as many cities as will let me book a tour. At my lover's insistence, I have spared no expense – rich costumes, elaborate sets, a stunning display. All of the glittering stage-effects of the popular play. But word-of-mouth has poisoned the box-office. Small crowds, unsold tickets, tepid reviews. 'The art of the great actress seemed paralysed by the character the poet drew with heavy stokes.' My lover sits at home and writes – and counts the money – and never reads a review. He never seems to want to come on the road. I have adjusted as much as I can – how far will he adjust to make our dream come true? He listens best when he has had his feathers smoothed. What soothing words – I wonder – will I think of to say when I get home?

One world approved your wisdom, another mine.

Friends, friends, friends. I have few friends and want even fewer. Does Electra have friends? – does Medea have friends? Nora? – Phedre? – Lady Macbeth? The others on the stage are merely the ghosts of the people whom they play. I have to act through them to get to the people of my story. And none of the people in my story are my friends.

Then

An actress who wears no mask and acts in mime.
Speaking at the speed of an author's pen.
Actors playing characters watching a play.

the dog's nose

Is it true that you choose your friends from outside the theatre?
Does this exclude both actors and patrons as well?

Why, may I ask, do you make such a strict divide?

wrinkled.

Tired and exhausted. Returning home much battered and bruised. I have given my very best. I have taken our plays all over the world. I have taken them to Paris, to New York, to St. Petersburg. It has been a difficult journey. Has my love for D'Annunzio carried me away? I suffered through some tough talks with a number of impresarios. Can we book another tour for next year? Not, my dear, if you bring these plays again. Future contracts sit unsigned. All is contingent on whether we do what they say we must do. Only then will these impresarios book our plays.

They all think that I am incapable of anything really serious.

You would do well to consider your loved-ones – Cleopatra and I. You would do well to know that the Nile is perpetual spring. Rome rises – Rome falls – the Tiber dwindles to a trickle. Come the spring, the Nile will rise and flood the plain. You think – and act – with the wisdom of a schoolboy. Cleopatra and I are telling you who we are.

Chapter 12

The bills pile higher and higher. The impresarios grumble and groan. You are paying a lot for your folly. Even your greatest aficionados are staying away. The popular press is hungry for scandal. They wonder why you so favour this man. He spends time with you and leaves his wife and children at home. The gigantic sets, the huge casts, the splendid costumes – so elaborate and such dead weight. Did you not realize that these plays would not work on the stage?

She could see herself sculptured.

Winning the audiences of Europe. Starting slowly and winning them over. A small house the first night – word of mouth and magnificent reviews. The next night every seat in the theatre is filled. Nora and I alone on the stage – we live in the theatre of Ibsen's mind. Not a word does Nora speak that I do not feel. The reviews are strong and fearless. Meeting writers and other artists. It is the young who understand what the two of us feel.

Sun on sails

An emery-stone sharpening a knife.
A person who claims to know the future.
A person who walks on desert sand.

or

Is this exchange not an interview under another title?
Is it not aiming at what an interview is designed to do?
Why did you not just send the young reporter away?

wreckage on rocks.

Real and living to our minds.
Feeling everything to a musical rhythm.
Persons we elbow in the narrow streets.

The young poet thought of the tragic actress. In her was embodied the essence of all the greatest roles. In her the fidelity of Antigone, the fury of Cassandra, the fever of Phedre, the cruelty of Medea. She has been Imogen, Juliet, Miranda, Rosalind, Jessica and Lady Macbeth. The tenderest, most terrible and most magnificent souls. All of Antiquity spoke with her tongue and flashed in her eyes.

He felt his head was insecure on his shoulders.

Tired, tired, tired of the same old roles. Mid-century romanticism at its worst. Cranked out like sausages by the likes of Sardou and praised – after barely a taste – by the likes of Sarcey. Wonderful roles for Sarah – filled with rainbows and thunder clouds. For me, there is little in these roles that is human. My most powerful lines as Marguerite are 'Armand – Armand' while he fills the stage with sighs and tears. We need an Italian Ibsen – an Italian Shakespeare. Where are the young writers who are capable of writing for me?

The girl had always trusted her father and her brother. She had felt that she would always welcome their advice. But both had voiced distrust of the prince's motives. Now the girl did not know whom to trust.

"She plays not-wanting-to think on the surface."
"She plays not-being-able-to-help-thinking beneath."

This is a puzzle that I must solve. That Aegisthus is guilty there is no doubt. Clytemnestra, my mother, is an enemy for sure. Circumstances urge me to act in the role of a god. But what will happen to me when the stage has been soaked in blood?

Pay for a mask - each one smashes to pieces - checking to see - a very useful intertwining - can make the changes - the person who is me - an unexpected quarter - lost my sense of distance - took separate ships - see it as a stimulus.

It is important for me to feel that you understand me. How could you write with conviction if you do not? That is why I have been rattling on in this vein.

Everything that I have said has come from a very deep place. That is why I have asked you to sit so close to me. That is why I have been looking so deeply into your eyes.

You are not the kind to trample on a flower. You are a person – I am sure – who has talent. Surely you yearn to do more than smear ink across a page. Have you ever had the urge to write a book?

On its shoulder a huge burden
was in place.

I am having it out with my lover. It has nothing to do with our love. Our plays have not been very successful. The soaring rhetoric, the grand gestures, the shockingly morbid scenes – reaching back to the romantic plays that are now out of style. They are more Sarah's kind of acting than they are mine. They are expensive, exorbitant, costly – requiring a huge crew and cast. They lose the audience, lose the reviewers, lose money night after night. The theatres, when I act our plays, are less than half-full. I am in love with you, my darling, but I am also a facer of facts. I must revive my old reliables – the plays that guarantee a full house. I will have to cut back on the number of performances of our plays. Now – this has nothing to do with our love – no, nothing at all.

The far-off brutal city black with coal.

The death of Cafiero. He who left me completely alone – alone in a fishing village with an unborn child. I shed a hundred tears. I count as Sarah counts when she acts in a play. A hundred tears and then no more. What I thought was going to be – and what turned out to be in the end. Who can admit what it is to be human? You can never weep for another – the human being can only weep for the self. I stop weeping for myself after one hundred tears.

She felt oppressed by her own personality.

I have not had good luck with the males of this world. We fly at different levels – we sing different songs. The female builds the nest but the male continues to fly. When he tires, he takes his rest on a cloud.

The young lady's husband felt compelled to turn against her. The poison curdled all the thoughts in his mind. For attacks on the mind the husband had no armour. The friend poured potent poison into his ear.

Finding the rope frayed at the well.
Plaiting it stronger at the spot where it was frayed.

"What do actresses do in their spare time? The public clamours to know. We know that Marguerite Gautier is a part that an actress plays. With Sarah Bernhardt we are always aware of this fact. She almost winks at the audience as she takes us through our turns. She is the rider and we are the thoroughbred making the jumps. And then when the weekend comes, we can buy the Sunday papers and there is Sarah reclining in the boudoir of a sumptuous villa in Paris or in Rome. Or in the carriage of a prince or a king or a millionaire. We read of her loves and her triumphs – of her kindness to those in distress – of her encouragement to her rivals on the stage. But of La Duse, there is nothing of this sort of thing. What is La Duse when she is not on the stage? A wife? – a mother? – an elegant grand dame? A femme fatale? – or a loyal helpmeet? Doesn't she know that the public has a raging thirst for such things? Give us some gossip, please, La Duse – we must imagine what we do not know. Do you think that all we want is to see you act?"

Some of the broken pieces - more a figment - to hold in her hand - a bird who flew so high - peering through iron bars - your hoped-for interview - relies on others - no going back - reach into the heart - dislodged from their carcasses.

Oh I could never be a journalist. I find it so painful to act in a superficial play. Surely you – with your sensitivity, with your compassion, with your insight into the agonies of the world – soar above the petty nature of your trade.

There is a thought that I have had. This thought has grown in me in the time I have spent alone. In my apartment, here in Venice, in my late-night gondola rides, in my dressing-room when I am exhausted by the life that I live on stage.

That I could right the wrongs of what has been done to me by the writings of someone else.

The crowds poured over the bridges
and rowed beneath.

The young poet thought of the tragic actress who had become his poetic muse. From that frail and slender body emanated the imperishable beauty of infinite worlds. The plains of Thebes, the olive groves of Colonus, the dark country near Dunsinane. Prospero's cave, the Forest of Arden – lands of blood and lands of pain – lands created by her on the stage with a frown or a smile. She was the soul of that ideal world. In the mystery of this living, breathing woman survived, for him, the power of primitive myth.

A river of blood has been shed for beauty.

Touring the cities of America. New York – Philadelphia – Chicago – Boston. *La Dame aux Camellias – Fedora – Fernande – Cavalleria – Locandiera – La Femme du Claude.* Full houses – warm welcomes – enthusiastic crowds. But oh, the assault on my sense of privacy! The constant requests for interviews! The constant thirst for gossip! Invitations to private soirees! Should I sell tickets to my boudoir? Should I hawk pamphlets on the street? Should I cancel the plays and lecture about my favourite drinks and foods? A lucrative offer to endorse a wretched local wine!

A person locked within a skull.
A slave girl who claims to know the truth.
A bed dressed with marriage sheets.

A great big eye – a great big massive eye. A great big eye, right here, in the centre of my forehead. One that would sweep around the landscape and penetrate the fog and discern the rocks and the shoals. A warning – to others as well as to me.

I hurry home and look in the mirror.
I cannot believe what I see.
Who is this creature in my mirror?
Why is this creature staring at me?

Is this 'non-interview' not one of your greatest performances?
Is it not, perhaps, the performance of your life?
Will you live or die when you read this young fellow's review?

I wake up and there is Romeo. He is dead and we are here, in this vault. Rose-petals are strewn on his body as he lies beside me. There are rose-petals on my body as well. We will sleep in each other's arms for a thousand years.

Here is where Juliet had her hair done.
It was the night of the Capulet ball.
Too young, she was, to expect to fall in love.

My rival is a fad, each thought. She is temporarily 'new'. Great art is that which lasts. She is chasing after sensation. I am crafting a whole career.

That which we see and can never have – that which we have and can never see. That which we lose and can never find – that which clings to us like a pestering burr. The jarring sounds that stifle the music that we so desperately want to hear.

Divining what will be said to us.
The depths of haunting eyes.
Art as tyrannical as imperious mistresses.

Two people lived as one – spoke as one – thought as one. Mother-daughter – father-daughter – woman-lover – woman-child. The sun rose every morning – the sun set every night. Between sunrise and sunset it was always noon. And even Death – morbid Death – was moved to tears.

My lover broods and broods and broods. He has had a terrible shock. He seems to have stopped his writing. I offer to help him to tighten our plays. They are a little too Sarah-minded – so much of the stuffing is only there for show. We can leave out some of the rhetoric. This is nothing new to me – I have adjusted many plays to the needs of the stage. I rub his temples as his head lies in my lap. We shall get through this together. I know a few tricks of the playwright's craft. Working together will serve to make our union strong.

Two people walking together on the grass.

I don't think about my mother – I can't. I don't think about my father – why should I? They were the best that they could be. Mother doling out the rations. Father coming up over the hill – waving his hat as high as he could to let us know. Acting! – money! – food! – warm beds! Father always walking ahead to scout a town.

The judge told the lady that he would solve her dilemma. He would tell her who was acceptable, in future, as company. The judge would tell her, in future, who was not. The judge would control those whom the lady was allowed to see.

"Transcendent genius, psychological power, magnetic force."
'You feel her eyes burn though the curtain after it's closed."

There is my daughter and there is my son. She is in love – he is in love. Should I choose my daughter's happiness or that of Armand? Life is a series of heartbreaking choices but I have managed as best I can. Only one will receive a bouquet and take a bow.

I have no idea - ashes, dregs and weeds - the brightest star - i am looking still - relieved of duty - exactly who i am - crush you in the shell - weight of my thoughts - i try to focus - no lack of nutrients.

I have always shunned publicity. I am not a person when I am not on stage. If I am not Hedda, or Nora or Rebecca, I do not exist.

Speaking to the public, in my own voice, to me is repugnant. It is hanging my washing out on the line. It is as if I am standing naked on the street.

But such is your persistence. Such is the quality of your writings that I have read. That – for this once only – only for this once – I will make an exception.

Dance and prance
upon the street.

She the actress of all the ages – he the poet of promise and youth. When they had first met, there was air and sunshine. Without speaking they had known each other's words. Their souls were ravished by the power of the eagle. They were bound together in the bands of eternal truth. All the melodies of the world passed through their bones.

A world diminishing in value.

Trailing around after Sarah – no matter where I go in the world. She is fifteen years older than I. She has been to every town. She has acted on every stage. She has trained the taste of every impresario, every audience, every reviewer, in her kind of theatre. I have to act in Sarah's plays – *La Dame Aux Camellias* and all the rest. Restage the Battle of London. Compete with Sarah's ghost. Prove myself – in every city – in the roles that Sarah has played.

The young mother tried to keep the secret from her husband. A man could never be beholden to his wife. She was caught in the forks of a dilemma. Finally, she was forced to tell her husband the truth.

Bringing the past alive in the present.
Wondering how to bring the present alive as well.

Oh you must let me paint your portrait.
I have a backdrop in my studio.
Some props that I have scrounged.
A costume and a hairpiece of my choice.
Your friends won't know the model that I used.

Before you trifle - none until i met him - a victory-lap - their blended souls - images of the ideal life - an element of your mind - such a strict divide - felt that they had met her - a person gathering baskets - manipulated their lives.

I have a proposal for you. That we two form what might be called 'a conspiracy'. But, in this case, a conspiracy of angels – bringing the truth – bringing the gospels – bringing the news.

That we tell the true story of these three people. Of Sarah – of D'Annunzio – of me. That we tell your readers the news behind the news.

So – take your pencil out of your pocket – or your pen – or your stiletto. Or whatever sharp weapon you tend to use. Dip it in lambs-milk rather than poison, as you usually do.

Be the clown
on the sawdust below.

I go out on the road again. A mixture of plays this time. Half D'Annunzio and half-popular, though I'd rather it were not so. But I have to pass the ticket-selling test. I wonder what my love is doing at home. I gently suggested he give up on plays. I sit down and write a letter. You are a brilliant, brilliant writer – but you are a poet and a novelist, through and through. I don't act parts that don't suit my talent – I don't jest in comedies or strut in male attire. Oh I love you for being so noble – for working so hard and doing your best. But you will be happier – love – if you put the past behind.

The beauty of the last twilight of September.

Why is it never enough? I see myself as the greatest actress of my time. Of all time, perhaps – how would one know? I can book a theatre in any major city in the world and act in any part in the popular or classical repertoire and have the impresarios, the reviewers and the public eating out of my hand. I give them the blood from my heart and they appreciate what I do. I return to my rooms with their applause clutched fiercely in my hand. And then I sit for hours and brood – brood and brood and brood – and wonder – why – oh why is it not enough?

The dog

A chosen veil of silence.
An actress's power wasted in a thin plot.
An elbow knocking over a can of paint.

sniffed

Are you sure that you would be keeping your deepest secrets?
Would his readers not be able to read between the lines?
Might you not, inadvertently, reveal your deepest concerns?

at the piece of meat.

But now, the young poet felt alone. The tragic actress had been Cassandra, had been Electra, had been all the greatest of classical roles. But she had spoken the words of others – of other writers in other times. Now he was perched on the precipice of a whole new world. She the actress – he the writer. How to find the words that would make the present soar?

The strength and the beauty of the day.

A photo of the poet, D'Annunzio, in the popular press. Short, slightly balding. An unprepossessing face. I should sweep such earth-bound concerns aside. He is a writer – an Italian writer. They say he writes impassioned, soul-searing verse. I feel the need to build an altar. To place a jewel in a casket that I can set high up on a shelf, where it will catch the first rays of sunrise at the dawn.

Chapter 13

A knife-thrust from an unexpected quarter. His book is out – his novel – and I hear disturbing things. Friends rush to me with copies that I don't want to read. The newspapers are filled with reviews – my pictures all over the pages. Vendors shout of shocking news from the grimy stalls. What do these vendors of scurrility assume that they know about me?

O, never was there queen so mightily betrayed.

Coming to the conclusion that what is needed – what I would love to see – is a whole new series of roles. I am tired of playing the honoured classics of the past. The popular plays of the present are all moth-eaten on opening night. For forty years playwrights have been copying Dumas-fils. Wilted camellias – tired situations – predictable words.

Sparkling waters

A person looking into another's eyes.
A shop with masks on all the walls.
A woman who watches herself give birth.

or

You have played, have you not, all the greatest female characters?
In all the greatest plays of the present and the past?
Do you have a favourite role that you love to play?

blood in the waves.

Folded in a veil like timid virgins.
Held beneath a yoke of power.
Knowing how to rend the veil.

No more adjacent villas in the hills above Florence. He has taken himself off to Rome. I walk alone on the nearby paths and mourn my loss. He has taken a knife and severed the cord that exchanged our blood. No more love and no more laughter. No more words of future plans. No more wine in the moonlight at midnight. No more song-bird outside my window. I am winter and he has flown to a warmer clime.

I go living to the vaults of death.

Slumped in a chair in my dressing room. I am exhausted before the play starts. Tonight, I am playing Cassandra again. We live – Cassandra and I – on a different plane. As if underwater – as if on a cloud. All of the other actors converse as if the world is a logical place. For Cassandra and I, the world is no place at all.

The prince was spied on by the young girl's father in the closet. He stabbed the curtain, thinking it hid the king. The girl's father died and left her unprotected. The prince lugged the guts to the neighbour room.

"Duse is an actress of extraordinary skill and power."
"A more nearly perfect theatrical performance is unimaginable."

I am sitting in a theatre in Heaven! I am the only one in the room! I can come here any time that I care to! I can watch my entire life! Every word I have ever spoken – every person I have known! I can watch my entire life from beginning to end!

In his mind crowded images - on an off-night - a hand on my shoulder - you are paying a lot - more of a contrast - in broken tears - the offending passage - the only path - no other choice - the power of primitive myth.

He wrote four plays for me. Each was shallower than the last. I took a turn at being Sarah – small performances and large applause.

Come closer! Move your chair closer to me! Lean forward – this is not for the ears of the butler or the maid!

Nothing of what I say must appear in print under my name! Do you hear? I forbid you to attribute to *me* one single word!

If you write any of this it must be under your own name! As *your* observations, after failing to get *me* to talk! You read my eyes, as you could not hear my voice!

It will be *your* opinion – *your* interpretation – *your* surmise – as to what I was thinking! The great lady – the great actress – the great Duse – retained her secrets on this topic of concern! Write what you like, but never attribute a word to me!

Put your hand on your heart! – do it now, before I speak! Not to tell – not to tell – not to tell! I forbid you – I forbid you – on your life!

Every once in a while,
the statue heaved a sigh
and shifted the burden
from one shoulder to another.

Why am I standing outside a bookstore? I have at least half-a-dozen copies at my home. My life, in a fiery pyramid, on display. Each page has been dipped in acid. Each word is a knife to the heart. Each anecdote has been turned on its head. Or so I am told – so I am told – so I am told.
There is no escape, friends, none when the time is full.
I will get no help from Sarah – Sarah revels in the tried and the true. New plays are written for Sarah which are copied from the old. Every Sarah-part is Sarah – warmed over from the play before. Every triumph is a victory-lap from a long-ago success. She will play the same parts when she is ninety. She will wring the hearts of her patrons every night in the arms of an eighty year-old Armand.

The young lady thought about her husband. The young lady thought about her marriage. She wondered whether she would ever regain his lost love. She wondered what her husband was going to do.

Feeling a knife enter my body – cold and sharp.
Feeling a hand reach into my chest and search for my heart.

My days in Heaven are long and thoughtful! I can sit and watch my life! As I watch my life I know what I know now! Many times I have tried to watch it! I have never watched to the end! I have only watched until I am Juliet!

Find the thread - the holes in your eyes - as fellow-watchers - natural flaws and wrinkles - the dormant dreams - every pimple and mole and scar - accept nothing in exchange - the bands of eternal truth - caused to be true - the ghosts of the people.

You know, he talked the novel to me – he talked the novel, you see. At that time – he told me – he hadn't written it down. All the time he was planning the novel – that is the time when we were hatching our Italian-theatre scheme.
Sarah was the older muse and I was the younger muse. He was inspired by her former glory, you see. We wanted to build a theatre – she was the older muse whose time had passed – the inspiration for it all – and I was the younger muse who would work the spell.
It's bait and switch, my friend – bait and switch. The oldest scam at the country fair. The oldest, most ancient ruse. And you fell for it with ease – you fell for it with ease.

But don't feel badly, my friend. Do not feel ill at ease. For I – who looked him in the eye – who scrutinized him night and day – fell for it too.

I felt a knife enter my back – between the fourth and fifth vertebrae. Someone told me that Sarah had signed to perform his new play. I denied the rumour, of course, but my heart skipped a beat as I read the offending passage in my faltering French.

He had stabbed me in the back. He had offered the play to Sarah. Our play – our child – our grail.

Sarah – the darling of the French. Sarah – who owned a theatre in Paris. Sarah – who held so many reviewers in her hand.

He wanted to take the world by storm. The theater-world was English and French. Where were his plans for Italian theatre? It was all I could do to take another breath.

The ancient paintings stood on guard
in their gilded frames.

He was a creature of my imagination. More a figment than a man. I wished him into being. Now I wish I could wish him away. He is the nightmare which I am certain is here to stay. I cut him out from whole cloth. Very few threads were original. It was I who made the puppet dance and sing.

Will 'a tell us what this show meant?

Oh how you mock me – oh how you mock me. You think that Cassandra is as mad as can be. I see everything in this room. I know every thought you think. I see time unfold in an instant before and behind. I knew you before I met you. I will know you when you are gone. I know the road you have travelled and when and where that road will end.

A look which nails the theme of a play.
Friends who do not recognize a model.
A woman who bellows the secrets of her soul.

Place your heart on the bedside table. Next your mind and then your nerves. Leave the clock in the sink – under water. Strip off your skin and leave it hanging on a hook on the door. Now – lie down and pat your pillow and lay your head among the feathers and go to sleep.

Now I am aging.
Now I am young.
Now I have wrinkles.
Now I have none.

What is your relationship with these characters?

Do you see what I'm trying to ask?
How much of yourself, do you think, is the audience privileged to see?

They are carrying me from the stage. The light of the torch comes through my eyelids. The smell of the pitch singes my nostrils. The burning flax crackles in my ears. A rose-petal tickles my nose.

Here is the spot where she first met Romeo.
They spoke their thoughts in rhyme.
One can almost hear the words of their sacred vow.

The tours continued. The fame grew greater. She performed throughout the world. People marvelled at her artistry. Every theatre was always filled.

There was a viper in the room. Who could have put it there? How did it know that I had an unguarded heart? How long did it snuggle in the blanket? Quietly awaiting its fatal cue? You told me you worked with pandas at the zoo.

Being led to a perfect life.
A soul filled with images.
A tree hung with beautiful chrysalides.

I was the butt of every play. I was driven mad in *Sogno d'un Mattino di Primavera*. I was blinded in *La Citta Morta*. I was mutilated in *La Gioconda*. He planned to bury me alive in *La Figlia di Iorio*. In every play, I faced death or destruction or decay. He made me ill, old, decrepit in every role. He was writing as I was smiling – as he sat at my desk in my room – and every word was a drop of poison in my wine.
But where, now, should I turn?
Where, I wonder, is the writer who will write the new classical roles? Plays with Italian settings? Roles with Italian women? Roles which will bring the Italian woman to the stage? Roles which I can play in my own language? Roles I can play all over the world? All artists create, but the exceptional artist re-creates. Oh where is the playwright who clutches the golden pen?

The woman's husband had no inkling of her dilemma. He was caught up in a muddle of petty concerns. The lady thought about the cage into which she had been maneuvered. She thought long and hard about what she could possibly do.

"Art is Bernhardt's dissipation, a sort of Bacchic orgy."
"It is Duse's consecration, her religion, her martyrdom."

Many times I flinch! Many, many times I flinch! I have tried to watch my life many times! There are no rules in Heaven! – I am never forced to watch! I could go on and never look back at what has been! Or I can watch as many times as I care to try!

Fell off the cloud - like hearts and like minds - you are the embodiment - illuminates every word - copied from the old - not always possible - shun all requests - not for us to do - they were still athirst - it is nothing to me.

I willed those plays to be the plays that I wanted them to be! I rose to my greatest heights! – I rose above my own possibilities! – I tried to make those plays the equal of Shakespeare and Racine! I fused my own blood and sweat and sputum with the playwright's paltry words!

I lifted D'Annunzio up by the scruff of the neck and held him up for all the world to admire! I shall make this man a god or I shall die! Take from me what you will! – I kneel at your altar with my neck exposed to the sword!

Make these plays – and this man – the equal of Aeschylus! – of Sophocles! – of Euripides! To this, ye gods, I pledge my immortal soul! Take from me what you will! – find in my innards that essence that came to me from your hands! – leave me broken here on the altar of the gods!

But, alas, it was not to be. A sow's ear is a sow's ear. There's many a woman who willed a man to be what such a puny man could never be.

And so, as you know, his plays were failures. Reviewers and audiences agreed. Undramatic, turgid, boring – not fit for the stage.

Sarah had failed – *I* had failed. The two leading actresses of the age. We had tried to breathe life into carcasses on the beach.

Well – who to blame? Who to blame? Should he blame himself – or me?

Maybe *I*, too, was an aging actress. Maybe *I*, too, was a fading star. Maybe *I*, too, was the reason his plays did not succeed.

Don't you see how he worked the ruse? It was simplicity itself. Whether he wrote while he talked to me or whether he didn't.

He was the young poet. *I* was the younger muse. The elder muse was always *Sarah* when we talked. And all the while – he was courting Sarah to act in his play.

Indifferent to the catcalls
and the applause.

Every play was written for Sarah. She the flamboyant – she the grand dame. She the exotic, preposterous exhibitionist of the extreme. I can see it all clearly now. When he was working at his desk. When he was lying on my lap. When we sipped wine on a blanket overlooking the town. He was hoping he could turn *me* into *Sarah*. He was writing plays that had nothing to do with me.

Heaven knows we need some fresh air.

You do not know me – you cannot know me. What I know and what I proclaim. I am Cassandra, the girl who is painted on the vase. A snake has whispered his truths to me. And I, in turn, have shouted these truths to you.

The young wife thought that her husband would be grateful. She had assumed that he would take the blame himself. But the husband was not grateful that his wife had saved his life. He branded her a liar and a thief.

Reaching my peak as an actor of the great roles of antiquity.
Searching for a writer who has talent equal to me.

My dreams of Sarah are pleasant and warm! I force myself to dream of her as the sun comes up at dawn! At the end of a series of nightmares that have kept me awake! I am a doll and the theatre is home! It is a warm and friendly place! There is no one in the audience whom I know! Not my parents! – not my lovers! – not my child! They have come for entertainment – to admire, to laugh, to cry! There is no one who wishes to question me after the show! Mechanical dolls applauding another mechanical doll!

Give myself a line - towers in the desert - a puddle of mud - inexpressible thought - a breath of fresh air - find in my innards - whether i should talk - we are all jailors - shake off the yoke - her seeds of hope.

Because his plays failed to take hold! That's why he turned on me! When the novel was actually written is not the point!

He moved *Sarah* out of the novel! He kept *himself* as the young genius of future promise! He moved *me* into the role of the fading, older muse!

He needed a younger muse, you see! One who had nothing to do with his plays! One who could still present the myth of his future star!

It was a simple bait and switch! He didn't have to change the names! Simply plant the rumours that you and the others have heard!

Sarah out and the Duse in! – Duse out and another girl in! All he needed was a rumour and people like you would do the rest! The names in the novel are 'Perdita', 'Stelio' and 'Donnatella', as you would know! He didn't even have to change the names!

Now – take these words and make them your own. None of this has come from me. If you say you are quoting me, I shall deny.

Say that this is *your* idea. Or – from an undisclosed source – a close friend of La Duse, speaking off the record – a wise observer of the scene. Or some un-attributable oracle who has divulged this information while under a spell.

Whose arms will be there
to catch you?

He has turned my life upside down. He has made me the aging actress and a singer the younger muse. Given Sarah's part to me and my part to some-one else. Was this true all along? – was he lying to me when he told me it was Sarah in that role? That I was the muse of the future? – the inspiration for the poet? – the younger muse? Just when did this base deception creep into our lives?

But 'Nora, Nora' is not so silly as you think.

Meeting the poet D'Annunzio. I meet him in Venice. I meet him at dawn, at the dock. High hopes but no premonitions. A fortune-teller is a role that I cannot play. Reaching a certain point in my journey. A position of weak-ness – a position of strength. A hole in my armour – an unlatched door in my castle wall. It will be the lightest and darkest period of my life. Is it worth my thinking about? Or would such thoughts be picking at best-forgotten scars? A stray puppy wandered out on the stage – and disrupted the play for a moment, to the delight of the audience – and then the prompter whispered the cue, and the play went on.

The dog

Attaching strings to a marionette.
Another person's blood in one's veins.
A thief who steals when backs are turned.

drew back

Do you take your roles off-stage when the play is over?
Do you know what I mean by such a question?
Do you sometimes think that you are still in the play?

and whimpered.

Sitting in my apartment. The windows closed – the lagoon is cold. The winter winds come off the sea and chill the town. A stack of novels on my table, beside my personal shrine. The gifts of 'friends' who assume that this novel is all about me. Are these the pages of the public mind? Is this the ink that colours their vision? Will my monument be this pyramid of lies?

Think you there was or might be such a man as this I dreamt of?

You are as deaf as Agamemnon. You are as doomed by what you don't know. None of my truths has brought me succor – my every warning has met a deaf ear. I am Cassandra who the children laugh to scorn. I am as doomed as your royal house – I am as doomed as your dog and your cat. But all of my truths will be revealed in the coming of time.

Chapter 14

Carrying on without him. Having no thoughts of what else I should do. Carrying on as if he had never left. Trying to strike a balance that I am sure would have made it all work.

Sparkling necklaces that once flashed their fires.

If we could only persuade the promoters – if we could only persuade the reviewers – if we could only persuade the public – that these plays are the first stepping-stones on the way to a whole new drama, which will someday be able to stand on its own. Mixing our plays – his plays – the D'Annunzio plays – in among the plays that seize and hold the stage.

The life of the theatre

A person who snuffs out a candle.
A person gathering baskets of pearls.
An exchange of the chemicals of the brain.

is always

What do you think of yourself when you are on stage?
What do you think of yourself when you read the scurrilous newspapers?

What do you think of yourself when you walk down the street?

the theatre of life.

Coming forth from one's prison.
Eyes filled with confidence.
A person who will never lose himself.

The young poet looked at the tragic actress. What did he see? – what did he see?

The intimate spectacle of the nuptial alliance.

The corrupt creature, the vagabond actress, the heroine of chance amours. The aging one who – in her life and on the stage – had belonged to any and every man. All the mire over which she had walked – all the infamy that clung to her shoes. An aging human – an aging human – after all.

The young girl mourned her dead father. In her grief she carried baskets of flowers. She sang old songs with bawdy lyrics. All eyes were sad to see the young girl rave.

"For Duse, a play is a vehicle for the expression of the absolute self."
"Duse's most powerful moments are those between the lines."

"The facts of the life of La Duse are meager and sparse. She has been married – but is not any more. She has a daughter – a girl of uncertain age – whom, rumour has it, lives in a convent and whom her mother seldom sees. She has her own acting troupe – and a very small group of close friends – and all are quite tight-lipped when asked about the actress's concerns. She was thirty-six when she met the writer of the novel and she was forty-two when they parted ways. No ages are given in the novel but, in actual life, the actress and the poet are only five years apart, according to the records, so it is obvious that the writer has exaggerated – by implication, in his fiction – the difference in age. Many of her friends have denied the validity of the fictional portrait, though the lady herself has been silent on the topic so far."

Almost hear the words - choose the roles - a make-shift platform - a comfortable grave - that which is expected - she is the rider - shallow-good and shallow-bad - exposed to the sword - such dead weight - a series of heart-breaking choices.

What have you read? – what have you read? Have you read the great roles? What would the great roles be for you?

How do you read? Do you read with your eyes open? Do you read with your eyes shut?

It sounds ridiculous, I know, but it's true. You must read in both these ways – both these methods – both these modes. You must read the great roles in daylight and in the dark.

A few cracks appeared each time,
and the custodians patched the cracks
in the marble of the statue's shoulders and its face.

He told me of the dead city – Mycenae. Not dead at all, he said. A city living and pulsing under the earth. It took a Schliemann to bring it back to life.
Words dissolved in insignificance.

It will take two of us, he told me – he to write and I to act – to make the present just as magnificent as the past. I listened, as he spoke, with tears in my eyes. Now – sometimes – in my darkest hours – I think of the dead city as myself.

The young lady thought long and hard about her situation. She realized that her husband was under an alien spell. She decided that she would rely on his better instincts. She would be loyal to her husband in the extreme.

Living in the aftermath of a hurricane.
Living in the aftermath of a typhoon.

Our little gift is ready for the Queen. Your asp is the symbol of power – over life and over death. Pharaohs know they should never stroke him under the chin. For whom does the Queen, in turn, I wonder, require such a gift? Take this basket and say you have brought a gift of figs.

Moth-eaten costumes - the rhythm of art - hands that were pressing juice - effaced herself completely - a great big massive eye - every brilliant moment - the torch that illuminates life - bargains like these - break my concentration - a lioness's will.

You must become that which you read. That which you read must become that which is you. You are an actor on a stage – an actor *in* a stage – and the stage is you.

You are the actor and the audience. Love yourself as Lady Macbeth – hate yourself as Lady Macbeth. Know yourself as Hedda Gabler – wonder, as Hedda Gabler, just who you are.

Did you not tell me that this creature – this fictional creature in the book – is feeling old? Is whiny? – clingy? – shallow? – insecure? Dithering? – vain? – ineffectual? – age-obsessed?

Unable to function without the aid of a male? Too old for the young protagonist? – too old for life itself? A spent artistic force? – a shrivelled dug?

Or was it told to me by someone else?

No, I haven't read the novel. And it is definitely not about me. How could it be when the writer hardly knew me at all?

It is a fiction. Pure and simple. Cut from whole cloth.

He has an amazing imagination. An eagle in full flight. From a drop of water he can make an ocean appear.

And every few years a new flock of children
appeared on the ancient streets.

The young poet looked at the young singer. What did he see? – what did he see?

A sybarite sleeping his last sleep.

He felt a yearning for her song. He felt an imperious demand for music. She was the necessary fuel for his life and his art. She was fresh youth – and maidenhood – and creative joy.

A creature staring back from a mirror.
A lady who is in danger of being ostracized.
A part which is given to someone else.

No drugs nor drink nor rationalization. Nor anything else that relieves you of the pain. Not even guilt, if it makes you feel better. No pride nor compassion – no kindness nor disdain. Not one crutch or splint or bandage. No suit of armour from the castle wall. Allow yourself nothing but the bluntest of truth. Now tell me – what do you see and what do you feel?

Now I am laughing.
Now I am crying.
The mask has nothing to do with my moods.
The mask has nothing to do with how I feel today.

What do you think of yourself when looking out your window on the Grand Canal?

What do you think of yourself during your midnight gondola rides?

What do you think of yourself when you are just being you?

The last rose-petals cling to my surplice. They are carrying me back to the grave. I will look up through the grass at the sun and the shade. A grain – an un-quarried diamond – a slumbering seed. How long before I will come to life again?

We tourists all stand on the balcony.
We all look at the orchard below.
We all imagine Romeo and hear his sighs.

She grew older – as everyone does. She adjusted her choice of parts. She never relied on theatrical makeup. She was acting with her mind and her heart. She was Phedre, Medea, Electra to the life.

Desperate for sadness – desperate for joy. Desperate for other people – desperate to be alone. Obsessed with an unanswerable question – how many candles does it take to light a room?

A person who bears his own destiny in his hands.
A heart faltering under the weight of pride.
The power of conferring divinity.

Staging the occasional production of one of his plays. One of his dull, drab plays – one of his stilted, unstageworthy plays – amid the Shakespeares and the Ibsens and the Racines. Paris – London – New York. Acting my heart out for tiny crowds. Oh I am stubborn if nothing else. Why, then, do I do this? – why do I try? Trying to prove, I suppose, that I was not star-struck – not a love-drunk maiden in thrall to an undeserving man – but that I was genuinely attempting to create an Italian classical theatre.

An intense exiled soul.

I try so hard but it doesn't work. The plays are Sarah-spectacle without Sarah's unfailing instinct for the needs of the stage. There was a time when I should have tapped myself on the shoulder – whispered in my own ear – told myself that the project was all in vain. All in vain. Yes, I can see now – all in vain.

The lady saw no way out of her dilemma. She was trapped by her tormentor in her home. He explained to her that life was closing in on her. Her father's pistol felt warm as she held it in her hand.

"Torvald moved all over the stage as he was speaking."

"Duse, as Nora, stood very still and went from surprise to disappointment to contempt with just her eyes."

"Little is known of the off-stage life of La Duse. She grants few interviews, and reveals very little when she does so. She allows few photographs of herself – off-duty as it were – in her home or in hotel rooms. Most of the photos that appear in the newspapers are in costume, as the characters from her plays. She never talks about herself as anything but an actress – as an interpreter of fictional characters on the stage. Perhaps the publication of this novel – *The Flame* – which some people see as the lady to the life, and other people see as absolutely false in every particular – will encourage the actress to talk. To come out from behind her chosen veil of silence and reveal a little bit about herself."

In the dark - castles guard the landscape - annihilation is the only word - our pact is of iron - the crushing hammer - doors that were open - the void lingers on - dead on the stage - turning out quite wrong - that mirror over there.

No. I haven't read the novel and will never do so. What did you call it? – *The Flame?* To read that novel would be to drink a fatal draught.

But he did read passages to me. When we were – let us say – on friendly terms. But – not the passages that my so-called friends tell me are now – it seems – so prominent in that book.

No. I don't want you to tell me about the contents of that book. I could read it myself if I chose to do so. But what I would like to know is this.

A person can steal a wallet. A person can steal a purse. We regret the loss, of course, but we don't feel that we have lost any part of ourselves.

But – and here is my question. A question that I am almost afraid to ask. This is why I have opened my heart to you.

We reach into a hive and remove the honey. We open a clam and extract the pearl. We pick a flower in the field and take it home.

Take the script and find your character;
take the words and make them yours.

The young poet felt the need of a younger muse. He was grateful to the aging actress – she had brought him to this high pass.

A symbol of his own ascension.

But the mountains ahead were rigorous. He would need the essence of youth. A new force – an unused weapon – for the next stage on his path. His head was whirling and he staggered and almost fell.

The young wife and mother thought long and hard about her situation. What did she owe to her husband? What did she owe to her two young children? What was the best way out of her dilemma?

Being pestered with visits from my friends.
Being pestered with letters from my daughter.

Oh you must let me attach these strings.
Every marionette has strings on hands and feet.
They will make you dance and sing.
They will make you prance and saunter.
They will bring you alive when the puppeteer pulls the strings.

I have no idea - nectar is poison - what would be best - the taste of
macaroons - i see nothing - they are unkind - the poetry and the poignancy - all
in my palm - the paper begins to melt - when the dark moods come.

But do you believe – now tell me truly – though perhaps I won't believe you.

Do you believe that another person – not with a knife or a sword – using something as simple as a book.

Can reach inside another person – reach into the heart – reach into the mind – and steal the way that person thinks of herself?

Who will you be there
to catch?

I am a piece of broken crockery, lying smashed on the kitchen floor. The table is set, the fire is in flame, the kettle boils.
The crew on the ship with the blood-red sails.
Oh what was the plan and what has transpired? What was the past and what is the now? What cupboard holds the bread – what cellar the wine?

The dog

An image of an actress poisoned by art.
Moving deeper into the self.
An actress seizing a character by the throat.

turned away

Does it matter what others think of you?
Does it matter what you think of yourself?
Or – is there a you which does not depend on thinking at all?

from the piece of meat.

The young poet lay in a swoon – his brain was racing at fever pitch – he stared, until his eyes ached, at the sky. To follow the pulse of my heart, to obey my innermost instinct, to listen to the voice within myself. To plunge into the fire – to find my bride.
A heart sinking like a stone.
A voice was speaking of the need for a younger muse. Put the aging actress aside – bring the young singer into your life. Steel yourself with armour of agate – the forces of destiny are directing you to that path.

Chapter 15

Lying dead on the stage – Marguerite or Cleopatra or Hedda. Lying here dead as the air-sawing thespians emote. I am as dead as dead can be. And there is no one who can breathe life into this corpse but some other me. Some other me who is not my current person. Some other me who I used to be.

Exiled from this land, a wanderer disowned.

Where is the Juliet that I was on my fourteenth birthday? Come to me – Juliet – as I lie here – and kiss myself awake. I wish to rise up and exit from this tomb.

There is life

An invalid left behind in a paupers' ward.
A mirror which distorts both height and size.
A reviewer who compares two performances.

and there is death

May I thank you for being so candid?
On behalf of future readers?
On behalf of all those by whom you are so admired?

every evening.

The awe-struck wonder of the sculptor.
Marble gods still warm in one's hands.
The perfect union of two souls.

No more D'Annunzio plays. I have tried – I have tried – I have tried. I have beaten the dead horse with a huge stick. The dead horse will not rise and pull the load. Sarah knew – she knew as soon as she stepped on the stage. She was only in thrall for a moment – a brief moment in the spell of the silver tongue – then she saw the mediocrity behind the bright eyes. She rolled the dead horse into the ditch and carried on.

I would give you some violets but they withered all.

I believe I was made for Ibsen. I believe that Ibsen was made for me. If only D'Annunzio had risen to that level. A shallow poet with the brilliant sparkle of tawdry jewels. But Ibsen reached down into the mud and found the gem and held it up to the cleansing light. Ibsen – the man who understands the female heart.

The male was always the bird who flew so high. He was always the one who had all the knowledge. He was always the one who had all the power. He was always the one with the brightest plumes.

"The scene with the father sent a chill through everyone in the audience."
"The death scene, a miracle of understatement, defies description."

It is the moment of my birth! My mother is thinking out loud! 'This is my daughter – Eleonora! She is an infant – newly born! I pray for her sun to rise each morning – I pray for her sun to set at eve! I pray that her seeds of hope will flourish throughout her day!'

Force myself to dream - look into your eyes - forgotten its innermost self - a smear of paint - that which we see - the first stepping-stones - the necessary fuel - i shed a hundred tears - to stand on its own - inadvertently, reveal.

Well that's all the time I have. I have other things to do. I never seem to have any leisure-time.

I have scripts to read. I have rehearsals I must attend. I have many things to occupy my time.

I assure you that I don't sit around and hope to be interviewed. I don't think of snappy things that I can say. I am too busy living my life to spend it that way.

The seasons passed and the marble statue
stood its ground.

Taking plays all over the world. Touring and touring and touring again. Playing all the parts I have played and always searching for something new. Every part has something to say to me – I have something to say to each part. Sometimes I caress the lady I play and sometimes she caresses me. Sometimes I seize her by the throat and sometimes it is she who seizes me.

Death is a favour to me, life is agony.

I am refreshed and I am exhausted – I breathe and I choke when I am on stage. I stagger into my dressing room and I sigh and flop down on my chair. I live my life over and over – I crawl over inches – I fly over miles. I am all who have lived and all who are certain to die. There is not a person with whom I do not share.

The female was always the bird who had no knowledge. She was always the one who had no power. Her flight-path was always an arc below the clouds. Her trajectory was out of her control.

Acting on stage and thinking of being in my apartment.
Sitting in my apartment and thinking of being on stage.

It is the moment of my giving birth! I am thinking out loud! 'This is my daughter – Enrichetta! She is an infant – newly born! I pray for her sun to rise each morning – I pray for her sun to set at eve! I pray that her seeds of hope will flourish throughout her day!'

Only fresh spring flowers - what token, what souvenir, what trophy - emerges from behind a curtain - that was her name - scorches on the page - the dog would wait - remember who you are - order poison or champagne - has never seen me - all the lightning in the sky.

I don't have any tickets with me. Otherwise I would give you one. Good for any play in which I can be found.

I would have written a note on the back. Allowing you to come backstage. Perhaps that would be the makings of an article all by itself.

People waiting to go on-stage. People declaiming and sawing the air. People flopping in a chair – exhausted – when they come off.

They sang their songs and chased the pigeons
in the square.

Why, I wonder, did I not shed a tear for Sarah? He spoke of the aging muse as he sharpened the nib of his pen. I felt that it was Sarah to the 't'. If D'Annunzio chose to be cruel to Sarah, what was that, I thought, to me? Only he knew what had passed between them and that was that. She had been cruel to me in action, as I had been cruel to her in thought. What his novel would say about Sarah was nothing to me. Well, we sow and then we gather. We all toil in similar fields. There is a harvest for every sower in every year.

I can hardly wait to see which of you shall win.

Judge Brack comes to see me. He feels quite welcome in my home. He speaks of a party that he monitored last night. Of a person who had no vine leaves in his hair. He speaks to me of his future plans. He speaks of the things that people will say. Of doors that were open that will now be closed. That he will be a constant presence in my life. If I were playing his part, I believe I would twirl my moustache.

Two people eating the same macaroon.
Adding water to make more palatable a classic play.
A Greek character speaking Italian in a French play.

Lazing and moping – moping and lazing. I laze around my apartment. I turn down dinner invitations with friends. Half-read books lie around with open pages. I think of myself as a bird in an unlocked cage. I don't know what it is. I shrivel up between engagements. I long to be out on the road. If I am not on stage I am not a person at all.

People mean well – I know they do. People tell me that my performances have changed lives. My life has been deepened by my performances, but it has not been changed at all. My performances have not changed Hedda – nor Cleopatra – nor Phedre – no, nor Cassandra at all. I wouldn't admire them if they turned their faces from the wind. But a deeper Hedda – a deeper Cassandra – a deeper Cleopatra – a deeper Phedre. Now that, I can admire. Give me the battered and bruised ship that keeps its course.

I never see myself in the mirror.
Always a face that I do not know.
Something is making my mask change faces.
The mask is presenting me to the world.

You have travelled all over the world?
You have acted the greatest of roles?
Now I wonder where you plan to go from here?

So this is how I am spending my fourteenth birthday – I am spending my fourteenth birthday as Juliet. I am born, grow up, get married and die the same day. I am spending my life as Juliet in the town of Verona. She is me and I am she – I have Juliet's blood in my veins. Cappelletto is my mother's maiden name.

We don't need to go into the tomb.
There is nothing there to be seen.
Juliet is not dead inside.

And all this time she kept her secret. Who was she when not on stage? She would always play a character. Did she have any self at all? Had she suffered all the pain of all those parts?

I walk around inside this skull. It resonates with the sound of the ticking clock. The room is dark. I see nothing through these eyes. Before the sun comes up, I will walk for miles.

The full value of that which is given.
A person who is lost to another.
Expressing one's consciousness of regret.

I have been something that I never thought that I would be. A person whose emotions have poured out over the borders of the stage. Myself as a child – myself as my father – myself as my mother. The males – doves and hawks – who came and went. My husband, Checchi – my own daughter, En-richetta. Every one of them was a character in a play. For only one person did I ever leave the stage. Or was it for two? Yes, of course it was – of course it was for two. Twice I lost my sense of distance and fell off the stage. And let that be a lesson for me. Never again – never again – never again.

Vienna – Moscow – St. Petersburg. Moving deeper into Ibsen. Acting in *A Doll's House, Hedda Gabler, Rosmersholm*. Bathing in the waters of the Ibsen plays – feeling the need for something more than the tried and true. Most of the plays that hold the stage are from the old era – they are Sarah's cup of tea. Broad gestures, elaborate costumes, shallow poetry – chanted or bayed. With Hedda and Nora I can feel myself come alive.
I shall see some squeaking Cleopatra boy my greatness.
I wonder how old Ibsen is – I would love a tour of Norway. I can see his soul in his writing. How wonderful it would be to meet the man.

But the male flew in the same sky as the female. He only appeared to have the knowledge and the power. He too was caught in the winds of a mighty maelstrom. In time, his vulnerability was revealed.

"There is nothing of the theatre in her acting."
"Duse is always the character that she plays."

It is the moment that I am in now! I am sitting in my apartment! I am looking out my window on the Grand Canal! What if I were to think out loud? – what are the words that I would say? Why should my sun come up at dawn? – why should my sun go down at eve? What is the moment at which I should aim throughout my day?

Resist the hand - can still see blood - a need to clear away - all imag-ine romeo - roles that i shall play - in thrall for a moment - carries it all inside - see it all clearly now - kindness, please - an actual person.

How many people live on this earth? Have you any idea? How many people are living their lives as we sit here and talk?
Ever imagine what they are doing? Of course, the earth is very large.

Everyone on the earth is living this moment at a different time of day.
Kneading the dough. Baking the bread. Wolfing it down.

Buying and selling. Sowing and reaping. Working in the fields or in an office in town.
Rowing a gondola outside this window. Scribbling in a notebook as fast as one can. Talking to a scribe who writes everything down.
I wish I could tell you of something spectacular. Of something I do that no one else does. I fall in the dust – I get up – I continue on my way.

Before the curtain drops,
be sure to take your bow.

New York – Paris – London. Moving deeper into Shakespeare. I thrive in the parts of Shakespeare – his female characters speak to me – but his imitators have the depth of a puddle, and the popular drama can no more stir my soul. Shakespeare alone in his boarding house – on his horse – or in a carriage – on his way to or from his home. What is he thinking? – what is he experiencing? – what does he know? Whatever it is, it is deep down inside him – waiting for him to dredge it up. Waiting for him to find the words that will make it soar and make it sing. I see him sitting in the candlelight after spending a difficult day. He pulls some paper out of his pocket and writes some words.
What's done cannot be undone.
There is no exit from the stage. Judge Brack has blocked every exit that I can see. Now, now, now, now, now. What exit do I *not* see? I stand in silence as he talks. He talks of 'valuable notebooks', of 'superfluous persons', of 'mutual understandings' while I think.

Look on the ground and you will see feathers. Feathers of the male and the female bird. Dislodged from their carcasses in the maelstrom. Some were destroyed and some were able to survive.

Acting characters and thinking the thoughts of playwrights.
Thinking of playwrights who never appear on a stage.

There was poison in her heart – there was a letter in her hand. She saw three faces as she looked down into the well. One was the girl of the song – one was her lover in search of a dream – hers was the aging face in a watery grave. The two had met – there was no going back – soon fate would bring the two together again. It would be an uneven struggle. She felt humiliation and defeat. Her future was, to her, an iron door. Lost love – lost love – lost life.

The same old roles - baskets of pearls - to concentrate one's thoughts
- nourished by a sunbeam - look for an opening - how does she manage - some-

thing that speaks - where i used to live - my blood in a pool - bombarded by every sensation.

Well – as far as I am concerned, you can write what you want. In fact, I'm sure you will. Ultimately, you see, it is nothing to me.

You owe nothing to me at all. Pledges have no guarantees, no matter what anyone might say. You can take the story of Duse and make it your own.

Alone – alone – alone. I go out on the stage alone. Alone when I sit in this chair and talk to you.

I know the things I know. And nothing can take them away from me. I will be clutching the truth in my talons as I lie in my grave.

Pity you if you sit in the bleachers
and watch the show.

Moving deeper into myself. What do these playwrights have that I do not have? What do these playwrights have that I need? What do these playwrights have that I am working my way towards?

I believe that before all else I am a reasonable human being.

Each has stood alone on a precipice, wondering whether to step – or jump – out into the air. I stand – alone – on a precipice of my own.

Then the dog

A character in a play without any friends.
A lady standing outside a bookstore.
A novel which is not about oneself.

turned

Your career is at its height?
You are, no doubt, in your prime?
Could I have a word or two on your future plans?

and ambled down the road.

Yes my daughter yearns for my visits – yes the playwrights send me their plays – yes the reviewers sharpen their pencils – yes the public place their pennies on the box-office counter. But I am me – alone on the stage – with all the emotions that I feel – with all the thoughts that I have in my head – with all the words of all the women who have lived before me. And I am the one who – now – is standing on that precipice. I am the one who is deciding whether to take that step. Whether to step – or jump – or soar – out into the air.

Publish the thing to the whole world.

I shall have to shoot Judge Brack or I shall have to shoot myself. It seems, to me, at the moment, that there is no other choice. Who are you to judge me? – you who hold me in your hand? Yes, yes – I see it clearly now. A moment of perfect clarity is mine. Yes – I have my father's pistol. I see now that I shall have to shoot Judge Brack.

Chapter 16

I feel a heavy weight on my shoulders – a weight which my other self is lifting for me. A snake which slithered onto my shoulders and circled my head. There were times when I could not breathe. The dead weight of my beggar-blind past. Carrying baskets in from the fields of my childhood and youth. Wilting in the shade of blustering males who soaked up the sun.

A face full of lights and shadows.

I have walked down many wrong roads. I have slept under orchards of trees with poisonous fruit. Now, I shake off the yoke of my many burdens. I stand – alone – at centre stage. Applaud or hiss at me – you see me, now, as I am.

Life and death

A story that begins in Vigevano.
A story that begins in Verona.
A story that begins in Venice.

in every performance

Do we spend our lives peering through iron bars?
Staring at keys that dangle on a peg on the prison wall?
What is the means by which we can open the prison door?

of every play.

A deadly blade palpating in one's side.
The chill of death cold in the hand.
Slipping out of the bounds of one's own life.

Oh I am a freed Egyptian slave. Walking barefoot over miles and miles of burning sand.

As you make your bed, so must you lie.

I look back and there is not one tiny D'Annunzio pyramid that I have helped to build. I helped him build houses of straw. I thought they were palaces at the time. They were blown away in a windstorm. The master had already left, so – after the windstorm – I considered myself to be free. I reach in my pocket for the compass that used to be me.

Flowers clung to the young girl as she sang in her watery grave.

"La Duse – the woman – has the lioness's pride."
"She is a woman of the senses – with a scorpion's mind."

As for
the child
in the desert,

My personal shrine - what i feel i must do - sparkling waters - will be
my hope - saw the mediocrity - which some people see - born, grow up, get
married - under an alien spell - hanging my washing out - reveals very little.

Well – so much for your hoped-for interview. You didn't really expect me to talk. This has been, for you, what amounts to an empty day.

Build a shrine
to what
you believe in.

My Enrichetta – my Enrichetta. I cannot drag her around on my travels – the kind of men who haunt the theatres are poison for a young girl.
One day, when the sun shone too brightly.
Perhaps a kind family will take her in – oh, I wonder what would be best? How can I know what would be best for my little girl? She is old enough to leave school – but what would I do with her?

She asked her maid to dress the bed with her marriage-sheets.

Sitting and listening to a young reporter.
Wondering whether I should talk to him or not.

She
managed
to survive.

Struggled out barely alive - not the shaping force - their range is in-
finitesimal - an empty day - deserts of indifference - i never read them - would

always protect - trying to forget - a shower of rose-petals - prefer desert sand.

What will your editor have to say? Will you be relieved of duty? Will he say you fell asleep while you were on guard?

Build a shrine
and fall
on your knees.

My mother, my father, my lovers, my husband – and Sarah and D'Annunzio as well. All of the actors in all of the dramas that I have played in the years of my life. All of these people who have wandered across my stage.
Mine own eyes were the evidence for what I saw.
I owe every one an apology – everyone owes an apology to me. Every one of us drank the poison – everyone sipped fresh nectar from the well. Every one of us played villain and hero – bandaged the wounds and plunged the knife. Every one of us should get down on our knees and scrub the blood from the stage. Every one of us should wash the stage with our tears.

A story with its gains and its losses.
A story with its highs and its lows.
A story with its ecstasy and pain.

You know, I woke up one day. We were rehearsing and someone said something and it stopped me in my tracks. We were rehearsing a classical play. It was early in my career, and I wasn't the lead, so I was expected to remain quiet and speak my lines when it came my turn. But I was stunned to realize that people change the classical plays to suit themselves. Of course, it's commonplace to me now, and I do it myself, but only in small ways. I add a small prop or invent a gesture. I did it with rose-petals – instinctively – when I played Juliet. I give myself a line to get me across the stage. But – to imagine tampering with Hedda – or Ophelia – or Lady Macbeth? Tampering with the alignment of the sun and the moon and the stars? I must go through what I must go through. Just the thought of it is enough to keep me awake all night.

I seek the shop where I lost my self-hood.
I walk along beside the canal.
I return to the scene of my horror.
The shop is no longer there.

Would you say that we are all jailors of other people?
Would you say that we are their prisoners as well?
Would you say that we are both at the very same time?

I have been Juliet for a day, and will be again. I have been Juliet in Verona – on the day of my fourteenth year. All of Verona has seen me live – all of Verona has seen me die – all of Verona has seen the tumultuous love that I feel. I do not exist when I am off stage – I only exist when I am on stage. The people of Verona have seen Juliet after all these years.

Juliet is not in the tomb.
She is standing here, among the tourists.
She is me.

I am me, she often told herself. The public has never seen me – on the stage or off the stage. I become Phedre when I am acting – Electra and Medea as well. These are the people that I have been instead of me. To the world there has never been a me at all.

What is the purpose of all this thinking? Of stirring the ashes in all these burnt-out fires? Looking for one little spark that still glows. Sensing the shadow of the cold on the frosted glass. Taking the poker and giving the ashes one final stir.

Transported into a kind of fictitious life.
The difficulty of willing oneself to breathe.
To contemplate the likeness of oneself.

The old gondolier plies his trade. I consider him as we glide from canal to canal. He is the embodiment of his craft. The sharpest eye – the steadiest hand – the sense of wave and wake and current. He looks to me, once in a while, for a nod or a word of new direction. Technique without emotion. Whatever thoughts he has are thoughts which take no toll. Perhaps I should have been a gondolier.

Perhaps I should write a book. Pour all of my thoughts into the pages and toss it into one of those grubby bookstalls that sell the celebrity-dirt. Or – perhaps I could chisel my thoughts onto a gigantic boulder and roll it down the side of a cliff and watch it plunge far down to the bottom of the sea. If I did, the sea would bubble and seethe and boil.
One that unconsciously drinks poison.
No – I shall never write a book. And – I shall never get rid of these agonizing thoughts.

She held the pistol to her temple as she talked.

"You will never get to know La Duse, as herself – as a woman."
"Just let that go and know the actress – La Duse – instead."

She found
light and heat
and shelter.

*Cause for concern - each is a rung - paid every bill - boulders down a
mountain - take no toll - at all introspective - who was never born - something
to look up to - the clearing skies reveal - has little right to be.*

You can tell him your pencil broke. Just when I got to the interesting
part. Say you'll try to remember every word I had to say.

Create the god
that you
are in need of.

Oh I am a piece of broken pottery. A vase with a missing fragment. An
errant elbow has inadvertently bumped the shelf.
Now, from head to foot I am marble constant.
I have been down on my hands and knees, searching the furniture and
the rugs. I am holding some of the broken pieces in place. Now I must find
myself some plaster and patch up the cracks.

She left the doll's house and slammed the door.

Looking out my apartment window at the canal.
Wondering whether I care to go for a gondola ride.

So it really
wasn't fatal
after all.

*Candles or coals - rickety stages, patched costumes, battered props
- answer the door - our eyes speak - the glow of the torches - revivify and redeem - not for one minute - back to his cell - drunk in the ambiance - turned
my back.*

You can make it all up from scratch. None of your readers will ever
know. When they've read it, they'll wrap the entrails, and throw it away.

The shrine
will be there
to comfort you.

I'll see my daughter – my Enrichetta. But what will I say? – just what will I say?

Who has told me all these things?

We are like strangers who meet occasionally – in the dark. The less she knows of my childhood the better off she will be – there's no romance in the ragged costumes and the rickety stage. Mother and daughter – mother and daughter – I have failed her in so many ways. I have no idea what either of us will say.

To this day

A story with sudden changes of direction.
A story with many beginnings and very few endings.
A story which continues on and on.

the girl

Oh where will you find release?
Will you find it at midnight in a gondola on the Grand Canal?
Or will it flutter down from a balcony and land on your shoulders and at your feet?

has never seen the dog.

The dead horse gets up and walks – yes, the dead horse gets up and walks. Perhaps I shall write a play – and this shall be its plot. With all of the poetry and poignancy of Shakespeare – with all the grit and angst of Ibsen – with all the anguish and the anxiety of Racine. With a stunning part that only I can play. With no makeup, no wigs, no false emotions. With an alternating rhythm of smiles and of tears.

And of this how much is believed, it matters not.

But this play – my own – shall have a dramatic ending. The dead horse – shall get up – and walk!

Three Books

Eleonora Duse: Let Me Have My Wings: a novel
Eleonora Duse spends her whole career producing, directing and acting in the great female roles of the theatrical repertoire. She claims that when she is not on stage, she does not exist. A poet publishes a novel in which an aging actress's only role is to be a young poet's muse. The publication of the novel is a crisis for La Duse as the fictional portrait of a pathetic, clinging female threatens to fill the void and become her personal myth in the public mind. But her greatest fear is that the imagery of the poet's book will alter the way she thinks of herself.

The Making of Eleonora Duse: Let Me Have My Wings: a reflective journal
This journal records the author's reflections on the process of the crafting of the novel as it evolved through the stages of planning, writing, editing and polishing. It constitutes an effort to be as conscious as possible of the process whereby the single idea that suggested the topic of the novel was expanded into a complex work of art. Topics range from the nuts and bolts of novel-building to the nature of the novel as an art-form.

Planning Eleonora Duse: Let Me Have My Wings: a planning notebook
During the writing of the novel, the author kept a notebook which records the day-by-day development of the novel as it found its shape and style. The notebook reveals how a vast cluster of thoughts was sifted, selected, structured and polished into novel-form.

The Project
Together, this novel, journal and notebook comprise the twenty-seventh installment in an on-going novel-writing project in which the author is exploring the concept of form and meaning in the novel, and of the novel as a form of expression in the 21st Century. All of the published journals and notebooks are available for free download at www.johnpassfield.ca.

About the Author

John Passfield was born in St. Thomas, Ontario, Canada, and continues to reside in Southern Ontario, near Cayuga, with his family. He is interested in exploring the development of the novel as an art-form, and has written many novels, planning notebooks and journals in his search for a form for the poetic novel of our time.

Novels by John Passfield

Grave Song
The Agony of Robert Chisholm

Jumbo
P. T. Barnum's Greatest Creation

Pinafore Park
The Swan Boat Incident

Water Lane
The Pilgrimage of Christopher Marlowe

Rain of Fire
The Ordeal of Conductor Spettigue

Victoria Day
The Fabric of the Community

The Wright Brothers
Flight is Possible

Leni Riefenstahl
The Valley of the Shadow

Out of the Park
The Cogitations of Babe Ruth

Raskolnikov
Murder with an Axe

Death Day
The Apology of Sergei Eisenstein

Einstein
Wonder

Geoffrey Chaucer
Canterbury Bound

Ospringe
A Visit with Grandad

Pompeii
Vesuvius Dominus

Beethoven
The Ninth Immersion

Job
The Cornerstone of the Universe

Bethune
The Only Person Alive in the World

Terry Fox
Somewhere the Hurting Must Stop

Lord and Lady Macbeth
Full of Scorpions is My Mind

Cyril Passfield
Out West

Glenn Gould
Light and Dark

Emily Brontë
More Myself Than I

L. M. Montgomery
I Gave You Life

Pauline Johnson
Know Who I Am

John Passfield
Saturday Morning

Eleonora Duse
Let Me Have My Wings

James McIntyre
The Mammoth Cheese

See www.johnpassfield.ca for publishing information.

In Search of Form and Meaning:
Journals by John Passfield

Each journal is a day-by-day record of the complex process that a writer undergoes while crafting a work of art. It records the largest decisions, of structure and theme, and the smallest decisions, such as the choice of one word over another, and the constant interaction between the two. Each journal is a record of a writer's reflection on the craft of novel-writing.

The Making of Grave Song

The Making of Jumbo

The Making of Pinafore Park

The Making of Water Lane

The Making of Rain of Fire

The Making of Victoria Day

The Making of Flight is Possible

The Making of The Valley of the Shadow

The Making of Out of the Park

The Making of Murder with an Axe

The Making of Death Day

The Making of Wonder

The Making of Canterbury Bound

The Making of Ospringe

The Making of Vesuvius Dominus

The Making of The Ninth Immersion

The Making of The Cornerstone of the Universe

The Making of The Only Person Alive in the World

The Making of Somewhere the Hurting Must Stop

The Making of Full of Scorpions is My Mind

The Making of Out West

The Making of Glenn Gould: Light and Dark

The Making of Emily Brontë: More Myself Than I

The Making of L. M. Montgomery: I Gave You Life

The Making of Pauline Johnson: Know Who I Am

The Making of John Passfield: Saturday Morning

The Making of Eleonora Duse: Let Me Have My Wings

The Making of James McIntyre: The Mammoth Cheese

Available for free access at www.johnpassfield.ca.

The Novel as an Art-Form:
Planning Notebooks by John Passfield

Each planning notebook records the planning, writing, editing and polishing of each novel. Each notebook is an attempt to record, understand, and organize the vast cluster of thoughts which occur as one grapples with the various levels of organization which a clear yet complex work of art demands.

Planning Grave Song

Planning Jumbo

Planning Pinafore Park

Planning Water Lane

Planning Rain of Fire

Planning Victoria Day

Planning Flight is Possible

Planning The Valley of the Shadow

Planning Out of the Park

Planning Murder with an Axe

Planning Death Day

Planning Wonder

Planning Canterbury Bound

Planning Ospringe

Planning Vesuvius Dominus

Planning The Ninth Immersion

Planning The Cornerstone of the Universe

Planning The Only Person Alive in the World

Planning Somewhere the Hurting Must Stop

Planning Full of Scorpions is My Mind

Planning Out West

Planning Glenn Gould: Light and Dark

Planning Emily Brontë: More Myself Than I

Planning L. M. Montgomery: I Gave You Life

Planning Pauline Johnson: Know Who I Am

Planning John Passfield: Saturday Morning

Planning Eleonora Duse: Let Me Have My Wings

Planning James McIntyre: The Mammoth Cheese

Available for free access at www.johnpassfield.ca.

Other Books
by John Passfield

Anthems I
Verses from the novels of
John Passfield

Oak Street
The Passfield Family

The Poetic Novel I
Influences and Elements

Intensities I
(1-100)
Verses on Various Topics

Intensities II
(101-200)

Available for free access at www.johnpassfield.ca.

www.ingramcontent.com/pod-product-compliance
Lightning Source LLC
Chambersburg PA
CBHW021733190726
48288CB00009B/3028